Critical Praise for Briar Ripley Page

"You're the monster, and you're human after all — all too human, yet something else. You have a special eye. It's not a way to see, but an emblem of what you'll do. Crave a meat that's yours and not yours. Bury the evidence. Befriend the dead. Itch to jump into your own abyss. Briar Ripley Page is grinning at us with this artful flesh-havoc. Their mood is contagious, and they send us into premeditated disarray.

"To read Lupus in Fabula is to be seduced and shocked, and then to become. Your breath becomes a whirr: plaintive, howling, splatter-Gothic. Try to explain yourself, and others will reply: "That's incredibly fucked up." So what will you do, body horror fans? Briar Ripley Page gives up thirteen tales that squeeze and sway us, we who have 'never been pure of heart.'"
-Tucker Lieberman, author of *Bad Fire*

"Lupus in Fabula is a gripping collection that will make you squirm with its unexpected and delectable discomforts. Page deftly crafts characters that are as alienating as they are relatable, and the results are astounding."

- Eve Harms, author of *Transmuted*

Lupus in Fabula

Briar Ripley Page

Cursed Morsels Press

Contents

Notice of Content Warnings

Content warnings for each story are available in the back of the book.

A Sign

Hi. It's me, the author.

In lieu of a dedication, I want to say that if you've been looking for a sign that you should transition, or make any other major change in your life (get divorced, move out, move in, have a kid, get a cat, switch professions, cut off your abuser, take up the violin), this is it. Go do it. There's still time. You're alive until you aren't.

Biological Reality

I can feel the creature curling in me like a worm. I can feel it sucking the vitality from my limbs, a great maggot stuck in the swollen meat of my belly.

I don't exactly feel revulsion, but it's very uncomfortable and inconvenient. What will happen when the little beast tears itself free, I don't like to think. I try to ignore its writhing, its sucking, as I push my squeaky janitor's cart down the hallway.

Everyone at work thinks of me as a man; they can't know about my little hitchhiker, my parasite. The nature of the parasite. I can't even tell people I have a tapeworm, white lie to explain how sick I've been. That begs the question of why I don't just go to the doctor, get some pills, flush it out. Well, I would if I could. I would if that were still allowed, still possible.

My coworkers think I'm getting fat. Or, possibly, that I have some kind of cancerous tumor that can't be removed. Possibly they think I'm dying; I haven't asked.

Possibly, I am dying. Sometimes I feel like I'm dying.

It doesn't matter. This is a mostly solitary job, and I can't afford to take any time off. My untucked uniform shirt, a faded blue and gray striped button-down, billows loosely over my abdomen like a circus tent. *Come and see the bearded lady! Come and see the pregnant man!*

Nausea tears through me like a gust of foul wind screaming down a tunnel. I retch and stumble, leaning on the plastic push-bar of my cart for balance. The surge passes quickly, and I recover. Only the pale, sparkling dots peppering the edges of my vision remind me that I am weak. Weak and sick.

This is the next to last room on the last floor of my assigned block for tonight. I prop open the door, get out my equipment, and begin mopping the laminated tile.

During the day, college students learn about geology here. There are rocks lined up along the windowsills. One is bulbous and marble-white, with chunky yellowish incursions that remind me of pus, snot, or vaginal discharge. Beside it sits the polished gray whorl of a small ammonite fossil.

Inside me, the creature writhes. I can feel its feet pressing on my walls. Its mouth sucking hungrily, toothlessly at my flesh. It takes everything. My own stomach growls as I make the geology classroom floor shine like the polished ammonite.

It's not like I haven't tried to kill it.

If anyone found out, of course, I would go to prison. Still, it's a risk I've been willing to take, at times. When I'm not in denial. When I'm not hoping the parasite will simply go away on its own. Hoping my body will re-absorb it somehow, clean and evidenceless.

When I first suspected, I drank heavily. I poured whisky down my throat like it could burn out the infection. I ate tissue-papery, poisonous flowers from my neighbor's garden. They made me vomit and had me hearing voices and music for a night and a day—terrible voices and harsh music, sounds that weren't really there. Only the creature and I could hear them. I wept, and the creature throttled my spine.

I didn't stop taking T until the prescribing doctor saw me a few months in and wouldn't give me a renewal without a pregnancy test. Nothing helped. It swallowed the liquor, the petals, the hormone injections. It swallowed everything, and it grew strong and wild in my guts.

My hands on the mop handle are all bone and vein. They're the hands of a crone. My arms are both too soft and too thin, though there's still enough wiry muscle left in them to slosh the soapy water around the linoleum. To scrub stains from windows and walls.

Hunger ties elaborate knots within me. I think of the old urban legend about tapeworm removal, how a patient would be starved for days and then have a raw, dripping chunk of beef waved in front of their nose and mouth. The worm, starved too, would leap straight up their esophagus to reach the feast, spooling out of their mouth like uncontrollable speech until it was free to die in the open air. Until it could be thrown upon the fire and burned to ash.

The creature kicks. It bears down on my private parts. Something thick and clotted spurts out of me, warm in my underwear. Cramps wring me like a used towel. I bend over and hold myself very still until this episode passes, which it quickly does, and I hobble my cart out of the geology classroom and into the next one. The last one. Thank all the gods and monsters.

This one's a biology classroom during the day. Things I can't name float in cloudy jars of fluid, their skin wrinkled and pressed to the glass. A poster on the wall shows the evolutionary history of whales, from delicate hoofed creatures to baleened behemoths and sharp-toothed seal-killers.

I remember Peter's weight on me, pressing down like the rock of his name. We were both so drunk. I was amazed he could get it up at all. In the dark of his parents' garage, lost in a damp haze of beer and Jack Daniels and early summer humidity, I could imagine we were lying deep beneath the sea. Ever since the new legislation, I'd only had sex with my mouth, hands, and anus. That night, though, when he pushed himself questioningly against my groin, I parted my legs and let him enter my body through the front hole. It hurt for a moment, the tissues unused to stretching, and then it felt good. Familiar. Waves lapping upon the shore of my insides. Nothing would come of it, I reasoned. It was just once. I was probably infertile from six years of testosterone, anyway.

But then the creature, quickening. The swell and the kick. The withering of my limbs as it sucked me dry to grow its own body. Peter long gone to other flings; I never told him. I've told no one.

Another spasm folds me in half before I can even start mopping my final floor.

A dark stain spreads over the crotch of my pants. The creature is slipping down, down, trying to tear its way out of me. Sooner than it should, but nowhere near soon enough.

Piss and shit dribble down my thighs without my consent. The whales and semi-whales on the poster swim through stifling, quiet air. I bite through my lip to keep from screaming and, delirious, lie down right there on the dirty floor. The mop clatters beside me.

I tear off my clothes and push, and push. More urine spurting over the linoleum. More black, earthy-smelling shit rolling out of me like a series of stones.

Nausea. I bring myself up into a crouch, swallow the vomit in my mouth, and push again. Again. Is anyone else on this level of the building? Can anyone hear me? Do I want them to?

The creature slides out from between my legs in a bloody mess. It's blue and tiny under all the filth, but it's alive. Its tiny fists wave feebly, and its gaping mouth moves. It's still attached to me by a long, fleshy rope.

Without thinking, I grab the rope and gnaw through it with my teeth, like a rat. I taste myself, and I taste terrible. Old pennies and latrines. Then I look down at the creature.

Some animals eat their offspring. The thought drifts into my mind as if broadcast from somewhere else. I look around the classroom for a radio, a projector. There's nothing.

Some animals eat their offspring. Like rats.

It's true. Nature isn't kind or sentimental. An animal can always make more babies, but sometimes it needs meat. Sometimes, an animal can't take care of its children. Sometimes, an animal is starving.

It's an elegant solution in its logic, its circularity. The infant subsumed once more by the body from whence it came.

My stomach growls. I have been so hungry. The creature on the floor writhes. My little worm. It lets loose a tiny, raspy cough of a cry.

It has been feeding on me for months. It has taken so much.

I could take it back. I could make sure there was no evidence, no little body for a snitch to discover in the trash. No chance of arrest.

Perhaps it tastes better than I do. Surely its flesh is more tender. It's ugly and filthy, but so are lots of things people eat.

Dizzy and gentle, I scoop the creature off the floor, which I will need to clean much more intensively than I initially planned. I bring its blue, bloody belly up to my face. My mouth floods with saliva. I open wide.

I bite down.

Appetites

I.

The madness grew first in him as a series of fleeting, inexplicable impulses, unbidden images like those glimpsed on the edge of sleep.

He thought of biting the butler, the new one his brother had recently hired, when the young man smiled stiffly at him. Red lips and ivory teeth, unmarked and unlined flesh with a glow about it like life itself. Pale, smooth. It would tear open easily.

And when that thought was shaken off, folded and put away, he thought of biting one of his brother's collies, parting its long silky hair and rending the skin. Dog's blood welling up in his mouth.

And when he shuddered and banished *that* thought, he saw a spider crawling up the wall in front of him and he imagined grasping the creature and tearing off each of its delicate legs, then shoving its plump body down his gullet.

The thoughts were, in a way, like the thoughts about men that had come first when he was young. When he was twelve and thirteen, staring at the veins in the back of the Latin master's hands. Staring at the gardener's dark member protruding from muddy trousers as the laborer covertly pissed behind a tree. The boy Renfield sat in the bushes as though entombed. Looked out through a frieze of branches that scratched him whenever he chanced motion. Was entranced by the arcing stream of urine, the gardener's bruised knuckles, the almost purple head from whence the urine came.

Renfield knew what he was, then.

He knew both that it was evil and that it was natural, that there was a sense and rightness to the thoughts he could not deny. Madness was the same—this other form of madness.

Renfield was much older now. He knew he must be careful to conceal the budding perversion, but he knew also that his family's wealth—his brother's wealth—afforded him a great deal of protection. If one was discreet, madness in the wealthy was a mere whisper of eccentricity. It would be politely ignored. One would not be sent to the madhouse, or to prison. One would not even face much social censure.

He would eat only flies, and other small insects. He could allow himself a few flies, when he was alone. He would not go to the butler, to bite him or to be bitten, to undress him or to be undressed. Renfield knew how to exercise self control, and this, besides wealth, was what had always protected him. He knew how to lie down in the dark and imagine, and be content with his imagination, and so he remained free.

If you can call this freedom, whispered a small voice inside him as he stared at the shadowed, vine-covered wallpaper in his bedroom, hoping another spider might come.

II.

The creature who came to him in dreams was not a man, although he wore a man's flesh. He wore the flesh of the most beautiful man Renfield had ever seen. Perhaps he was an angel, like Lucifer. Red lips and ivory teeth, the canines long and thin like the teeth of a great cat. Pale, smooth skin with a glow about it like life itself. Chiseled features, simultaneously hawk-ish and leonine. Long fingernails that curved like claws. Every-thing about the angel was gloriously predatory, and Renfield trembled before him, waiting to be ripped to pieces.

Instead, the angel smiled at Renfield. It was not a kind smile; the angel, Renfield knew, was incapable of real kindness. But it was a smile of understanding, a smile of invitation. The angel's eyes gleamed in the dark as a great cat's would.

For many months—for many years—that was all. The angel smiled at Renfield and vanished again into the swirling chaos of Renfield's dreaming. There was no rending of flesh, no press of lips and teeth, no word passed between them.

But those smiles strengthened Renfield. He woke knowing he was not alone, that he would never be truly alone.

III.

Flies and spiders, and once a mouse he ate in two bites, head-first. He liked the way its bones felt in the cave of his mouth, but it wasn't as fortifying as he'd imagined; hardly better than the flies, really. It seemed that carnivorous animals, like spiders, offered more energy, more power, more satisfaction.

That was perfectly logical, when Renfield considered it. By devouring an animal that had supped on other animals, was he not consuming all the lives it had consumed in its turn? Many in one. Efficiency.

He could, he realized, start a sort of spider farm: capture flies and other insects, feed them to the spiders. Encourage the spiders to trust him, to grow huge. Harvest them when they were ready.

No one visited Renfield's room but the servants, and very occasionally his brother. The servants would be difficult to keep out, but not impossible. Some he could bribe or cajole; others, he could threaten.

His brother he would simply chance; his visits were so seldom, and besides, they were family. One of their mother's deathbed commands was that Renfield's brother continue looking after him, caring for him.

Bartholomew wouldn't take Renfield's spiders from him, surely. He wouldn't divest his brother of his quiet vices, his little fantasies. Surely.

IV.

The angel had been visiting Renfield's dreams since he was still a young man, but he did not speak until Renfield had begun to make the necessary preparations for his spider farm.

"Well done," said the angel, in a mellifluous baritone. He had a faint accent Renfield could not place. "You are finally progressing." His teeth flashed and his cloak billowed, though in the dream there was no wind. "Tell me, then, what is the mightiest carnivore of all? What creature would give you the most life, the most power?"

Renfield's knees shook with dread and desire. He found it difficult to think in the angel's presence, but the question did not seem rhetorical and he thought it would be rude not to venture any answer. He looked around the graveyard, for in this dream they stood among tombstones on a high hill. Beyond the cemetery gates were tall pines, closely clustered: a forest. Renfield heard howling from somewhere far away.

"A wolf," he guessed, and then he thought of the angel's eyes flashing in the dark. "Or a tiger, perhaps."

The angel laughed. It was a beautiful, terrible sound. "Not a tiger," he said. "Lucky for you and lucky for me. Tigers are quite difficult to come by these days, and I imagine that difficulty will only increase in the future. No, I speak of the only beast that hunts tigers, the only beast that hunts wolves, the only beast whose appetite is truly bottomless. The beast who devours all the world. I speak of man."

Renfield's mouth was dry. His heart beat so quickly in his chest. His head felt so light and expansive. "Man," he whispered. "Master, I cannot."

He had never called anyone Master before, and the angel had not asked him to do it.

"But you want to," said the angel. "Thirty years and more you have desired the taste of man's flesh. Do you know what that makes you?"

Renfield thought he did, but he would not say the word. He shook his head.

The angel's cloak swirled about his fine, strong limbs, and the angel's eyes flashed, and a fork of lightning made its swift, jagged, silent way across the indigo sky.

"You are the most human of all men, Robert Martin Renfield. The Ur-Man. The apex devourer."

"Master," whispered Renfield, "I cannot succumb to these urges. I must content myself with the spiders. Perhaps, one day, I might work my way up to a ... to a rat, perhaps, or even a cat. But I must leave men alone. They'd lock me away, you understand."

"You lock yourself away!" rumbled the angel. "You fear bars of iron so much you make a prison of your brain, your body, your little life in your brother's mansion. Deny your nature if you please, but the blood will work its power, and your heart will seek its proper course, and I will be there when it does."

He pulled his cloak about him and was gone.

V.

The spiders grew in size and number. They spun their webs across the walls, across the furniture, across Renfield himself as he slept. He ate them daily, and his strength increased, and he began to take on the look and stride of a younger man. No one came into his room.

All was well for a month, six months, a year. More than a year.

Renfield attended to his duties, and ate ordinary food at mealtimes, and did not trouble his brother or his brother's family. If anyone suspected something amiss with him, they never said so.

But as the seasons crept past, Renfield's hunger grew. He thought more and more often of eating rats, cats, dogs. Men. The angel visited him in his dreams almost every night, and the angel told Renfield he must inevitably take these next steps. The angel showed him oceanic tides of blood and cities built of bone. The angel caressed Renfield's skin with his claws, and put his sharp teeth to Renfield's throat, but he would go no farther. Renfield begged silently, knowing the angel heard his desire as well as if he'd shouted it. His body felt like a hollow chamber filled with clouds of winged insects, filled with every life he'd ever eaten stirred to furious motion, glimmering through his dark interior. His cock stood, ached. What if he were free to do as he pleased? Exactly as he pleased?

"You are not ready for me yet," the angel said, each time. "You know what you must do to be ready. The time will come."

Renfield woke before dawn, bereft, brushing strands of spi-der-silk from his limbs. He crowded a few large spiders into his mouth and chewed them. They were squishy and sour. They did not satisfy. What was he doing, eating spiders like a bird or a snake? He was a man. He would be more than a man. The angel would come and take him away.

Renfield's hand wandered beneath his nightshirt. He stared at the wall before him, trying to see the vine-patterned paper through the crawling, creeping, buzzing life teeming up and down its surface. Through the dust and the spiderwebs.

A face took shape in the dark pool of his mind. Red lips and ivory teeth. A glow like life itself. At first, Renfield mistook it for the angel. Then he realized it was his brother's new butler. Not so new anymore, now, but still young. Still handsome. Still glowing.

Surely the resemblance was more than coincidence.

Surely this was a sign.

The butler was only a butler, and he was not even particularly good at his job.

It was a risk, but it was a risk Renfield knew he had to take. As he finished into his dirty sheets, he thought of sharp teeth piercing his flesh, rending him, dividing him, and making him anew.

VI.

The butler was lazy, it was true, and careless, with a half-con-cealed taste for drink and pinching maids' bottoms, but he was physically much stronger than Renfield expected. Not as strong as Renfield himself, but strong enough to briefly gain the upper hand, push his slavering assailant off him, and flee the room.

Perhaps, Renfield thought later, things would still have been all right if he'd kept calm during the next few minutes. Perhaps he could have removed most of the spiders and insects from his chamber, or hidden them somehow. He could have said the butler was lying, or had misunderstood his intentions and started a fight. Who would people believe? The butler was only a butler. He was not even particularly good at his job. The maids could attest to his low character.

But perhaps, Renfield would admit to himself from the confines of Seward's asylum, part of him had wanted to be caught. Had wanted to be stopped from crossing the line between madman and murderer. Had wanted to have his power of choice taken from him by doctors and iron bars and the law, rather than by the angel's implacable logic, the angel's persistent seduction.

So Renfield ran after the butler, knife in hand, spittle and shouts flying from his mouth. He slashed furniture, wallpaper, his brother's wife's dress. He bit one of the collies. He fought the servants who tried to subdue him—two, three, four of them. He fought his own brother, when Bartholomew joined the fray, and it was Bartholomew who brought him down and tied his arms and legs, then set him on a chaise longue and forced laudanum down his throat until he was quiescent.

"Why, Robbie?" Bartholomew asked, as they waited for professional men to come with their legal forms and their straitjackets and their locks and their keys. "Why would you do such things?"

Renfield was so drugged he could barely answer. "Life," he said, as the world blurred and swam. He knew his brother would not understand. "Life, and freedom. To become ..."

VII.

"So, at the last, you failed," said the angel. His eyebrows were stern, though his voice betrayed no anger. No particular disappointment. "You may not be ready for some time yet."

"Please, Master." Renfield reached out. He went down on his knees. His fingers brushed the old velvet of the angel's cloak. "Please. They've locked me away at last. Don't abandon me now. Don't drive me to despair."

The angel slowly shook his magnificent head. "Of course not. I still have use for you. Later. We both must wait."

Renfield's knees sank into the cold, damp earth. They were in the graveyard, as they so often were, and it was night, as it always was. A smell like iron rose from the soil. "Please, Master. Give me something. Some token to show me you are no figment of my madness. Please. The asylum is very lonely, and I am left far too much with my thoughts."

The angel laughed. He grabbed Renfield's neck in one big, clawed hand and pulled him to his feet. Pulled him forward. Drew him behind the velvet cloak. "What would you have?"

His body was as pale as a corpse, or a marble statue atop a tomb. His body was as muscular and sinewy as a tiger's, or a wolf's. Renfield, his neck still squeezed, his breath choked out of him, could not speak a word in reply.

It didn't matter. The angel knew.

Swallow Me (W)hole

June 6

Practice today. Cyra and Trevor fighting again; Zissi and I ignored them. New songs coming along okay. Cyra liked my improv on "Nail Through the Palm." Trevor said I was showboating, but I think he just wanted to make Cyra mad. I don't showboat. Don't like the attention; they know that. Cyra kept trying to take video for her Instagram, and I brushed all my hair in front of my face. If I could've ducked under the keyboard, I would have. If they could've played the song without me, I would've left until she put her fucking phone away. Cyra and her sequins, her silver lips, her artful, calculated filters and hashtags and whatnot. Cultivating her band as brand.

... Shouldn't be such a bitch, even in my private notebook. Cyra's cool. Cyra's a normal person, with social media accounts and friends and ambitions and a partner—though I'm not sure how long she and Trevor are gonna last at this rate. Or what it'll mean for Virginia Fur if they split. I'd have to find another gig, I suppose, but I like this one. I'm used to it, at least—it's been steady work for months now. Cyra's a trust fund baby, and she pays a lot better than taking piano requests at hotel bars.

And I like Zissi. We play well together. Wish she talked more. I'm no good at talking to people, but if she talked to me, I'd listen. She's prettier than Cyra, and her voice is better, too, but she's shy. Sensible shoes, sensible bob, no tattoos or fishnet. I feel we've made a real connection, though. Her cello, my keys. We converse with strings, with bow and hammers, notes and chords. It's a language more comfortable than words.

It's starting to get so humid at night. Moisture like a big animal licking me all over. Gives me the weirdest dreams.

June 8

Woke up sticky. Get your mind outta the gutter, diary—it's the damn weather. I got my box fan going right next to the bed, but it's not enough. I need a dehumidifier, but I'm broke. That old hospital-green paint is peeling off the walls, especially up near the ceiling. Reminds me of diseased skin. The bread I bought two days ago already moldy.

Hauled myself upright to take a cold shower, trying to remember my dreams. Had a dull headache, beer hangover most likely. I don't go out much, but it's hard to sleep without three or four drinks in me, anymore. I read somewhere that alcohol inhibits dreaming, something about neurotransmitters and sleep cycles. Try telling that to my brain. Every night, I'm lost in these phantasmagoric sensory landscapes. Sometimes they're pleasant. Sometimes I hear music that melts my insides into, just, this jelly of rapture. Sometimes—okay, *usually*—they're worse. Broken glass puncturing me, hands all over, dirty fingers jammed in my mouth, in my crotch, in the cartilaginous spaces between my vertebrae. Everything thick black and shiny green, humming like flies. I think there are stories to these dreams, but once I'm fully awake I can only recall fragments.

So I'm standing in the shower, letting the water hit me right at the nape of my neck, rubbing pine tar soap all over myself, when I see that I'm hurt. There's a hole in my chest, set right smack between my breasts at nipple-level. It's tiny, like a zit, but it's definitely a *hole*—some kind of puncture wound, I guess. Perfectly round. It's not bleeding, and I don't feel any pain, but the edges are super inflamed, bright red and puffy. The contrast between edge and interior makes the hole look pitch dark.

I poke at it a little, and it stings bad enough that I don't try that again. I have a crazy thought that in my dream last night I was being chased by this gigantic insect, this thing like a big butterfly or moth, and when it caught me, it lanced me with its proboscis. Right *there*, right where that puncture wound is now. At first I'm like, *Get real, Maureen. This isn't a movie in the Nightmare on Elm Street franchise. Things that happen in dreams can't injure you in real life.* But then it occurred to me, of course, that something happening to my sleeping body in real life could affect the content of my dreams.

I think maybe a bug bit me. Or a spider. Debating whether to consult Dr. Google on this one, but searching for my symptoms, or for a list of venomous insects in my area, would probably just freak me out and convince me that I'm dying. Anyway, I don't have health insurance now that I'm 26. I'll wait a few days and see if it gets better or worse before I decide anything. In my experience, 90% of health problems eventually go away if you just pretend they're not happening and leave them alone. And the other 10% are all in your head. Ha-ha.

June 9

Practice today was a shitshow. Trevor kept picking and picking at Cyra, criticizing her voice, her lyrics, her outfit, until she finally blew up and yelled at him. Told him if he was so unhappy with Virginia Fur, he could fuck off and start his own band. She spit at his feet on the cracked cement floor.

He called her bluff. "Okay," he said, "let's see how well you do without a drummer. You think I'm expendable, but I'm not. Now get the hell out of my dad's garage."

Zissi and I looked at each other all nervous. Her eyes were big and soft and shocked. Trevor glanced at us and said, voice dripping condescension, that we shouldn't worry, that we'd be fine, that Cyra had enough money to rent a better practice space and if we were smart we'd be leaving the band soon anyway because it was nothing more than a talentless rich girl's narcissistic rock star dress up game.

Cyra took a step towards Trevor, her hands up in a truce-calling gesture and her mouth open like she was about to say something, but he didn't let her speak. "Get out," he said quietly, pointing a finger at her. "All of you. Leave *now*."

So we left. Cyra said she'd try and talk him out of it. Failing that, she'd find a new practice space, rearrange some of our songs. We have a show booked next week, but she's sure everything will end up okay. Zissi tried to comfort her; she shrugged it off. Acted like she wasn't upset at all, but I could hear her voice get thick and shaky with emotion. Poor, silly Cyra.

My chest itched like crazy where the bug bite was, and I kept scratching and scratching through my shirt during that whole conversation. Didn't even realize I was doing it until they both looked my way and Cyra said, "Jesus, Maureen," and Zissi asked me if I needed her to go over to Walgreens for some bandages and hydrogen peroxide. I noticed my fingers were wet and sticky, and when I looked down, blood was seeping through the fabric of the shirt. Big spreading stain with a circular indent in the middle marking the wound. Maybe it was my imagination, but it felt like it was sucking at my fingertips through the blood. Pulling them towards it. Greedy little mouth.

Of course, I was freaked out and embarrassed. I told them it was nothing, just a cut I'd gotten the other day that must've opened back up because I kept messing with it. Hurried home as fast as I could and ran straight to the bathroom to clean it off. God, Zissi was so nice, but her *face* ... she had this absolutely *disgusted* look, like I was an insect. Like I was some kind of horrible giant bug. I never want her to look at me that way again.

Weird thing: turns out all the blood was from my scratching around the wound. The hole itself is still neat and black, not bleeding at all. Not oozing pus. Nothing like that, except. Except I'm almost positive it's bigger than it was yesterday? It was the size of a zit; now it's a little wider than a pencil eraser. It's *really dark* inside the hole, darker than it should be. I ought to be able to see some red, right? Some flesh colors? But no. It could be deep space in there.

Anyway, I seriously dug into myself. It's nasty. Haven't pulled that sort of stunt in a while, but I did used to have a real thing with picking at scabs and popping zits. *You* know. I put Bactine on the scratches and then a gauze pad over hole and scratches alike, taped down firm. I'll give it another day or two for observation and then go see a doctor if it's still like this.

June 10

Well, I won't be going to the doctor. Fuck. Okay. I have to try to write this down.

~~It's fucking insane. I don't understand what could possibly~~ ~~Someone wake me up~~

Okay. Okay, okay, Maureen. We're *not* getting hysterical. We're writing this shit down. Writing can help us make sense of things. Remember what the shrinks told you.

Breathe in and out. In and out.

Here's what happened:

I woke up this morning (still sweating like a hog, thanks), and the gauze pad was gone. The tape was gone. Most of the worst scratches on my chest were gone, too.

The hole had eaten them all. It had eaten them, and it had grown.

It's more than an inch and a half wide now. I measured, and then it sucked the tape measure out of my hand, pulled it into itself. I saw the tape measure unspooling, falling, falling a long, long way, like down a mineshaft, until it disappeared. Impossible, of course. I'm not that deep. And yet I watched it happen.

When the tape measure was gone, the hole was just a little larger than it had been before. That's why I write "more than an inch and a half." Ha. All measurements will have to be approximate from now on, diary. Sorry.

The hole takes up space on my chest; it pushes my breasts out a little to either side. I still can't feel it, apart from those itchy edges. Where the hole sits, there's nothing, no sensation, not even a sensation of numbness. It's like it's not a part of me at all.

Maybe it isn't. Fuck. I don't know. It doesn't lead inside my body, that's for sure. The interior of the hole is clearly visible now, and it's still dark, all black. Smooth, no meat or bone to speak of, but with a depth to it, somehow, even without any objects falling through it to give a sense of perspective. It looks like it goes on forever.

It's *hungry*, too. I can feel its suction, the no-sensation eating at the edges of itself, pulling on my hands and the ends of my hair when I'm not careful. I don't dare try and put on a shirt. Leaving the apartment is completely out of the question. I've been sitting in the middle of the floor all day, drinking fucking Genesee Cream Ale like it's water. (Frankly, it might as well be.

Three cans in, and I'm still sober as a Mormon missionary.) Sweating it out, staring at the peeling walls. Wondering what the hell I'm supposed to do now. Hoping this is another one of my nightmares.

June 12 or 13, I think

I've been playing the keyboard. Virginia Fur songs, first: "Garbage Sucker", "Celestial", "Eat My Liver", all the ones with complicated parts for me. When I get tired of that, I play my old karaoke night favorites. "Creep", "Violet", "Against Pollution", more embarrassing stuff. My downstairs neighbor bangs on the ceiling, but fuck him. This is the last thing I have to keep myself from losing it completely. Apart, I suppose, from writing in here.

All the booze in the apartment is gone. I drank until I passed out. When I woke up, after I could open my eyes again, I examined the hole in my chest and went back to the fridge for the rest of my beer. Then the half-empty bottle of vodka I keep under the sink, mixed with orange juice. The hole keeps growing, mostly slow and steady, but faster when I was drunk enough to think that feeding it my crushed beer cans would be a funny idea. It swallowed them as easily as it did the tape measure, and I watched them swirl away into the void like tiny sparkling UFOs.

The hole is about as wide as my fist now, about the width of my heart. I don't understand how I can be alive with this thing in me, but alive I am. Haven't been eating much. I don't feel hungry at all. ~~Maybe the hole eats for me, now. Maybe the hole is something new that I'm becoming, the way larvae become winged insects. Or maybe the hole is something eating me, as much as it eats the things that fall into its small gravity. Maybe it's like one of those parasitic wasps that incubate in the bodies of spiders.~~

~~(Yeah, I watched a lot of nature documentaries when I was in the hospital. *You* remember. And yeah, I've considered that maybe I'm just crazy again, too. But this feels so real, and I never had hallucinations or delusions before. They said it was depression and PTSD. And self-mutilation. Excuse me, "body-focused repetitive behavior.")~~

I keep thinking about that dream I had, however many days and nights ago. The insect proboscis penetrating me. Did it leave something behind, besides a wound? ~~An egg? A child?~~ Fuck, *now* I sound crazy.

My phone's been blowing up, of course. Cyra and Zissi and even a few messages from Trevor. One from Mom. One from my brother, but he just wants to borrow money, as usual. (Like I have money to spare, Dylan.) I read them all, but I don't answer any of them. What could I possibly say?

I hope nobody comes looking for me. I hope they'll be able to let me go without too much fuss. I think they will. I think so. Who visited me in the hospital, after all? Just Mom, and she came less and less often after the first month. I've always been disposable. Not beautiful, not pleasant, not exceptionally talented. Nobody looks at me twice, unless it's to sneer or cringe. Nobody remembers me for long once I've left a room.

The darkness of the hole seems to pulse whenever I stare into it too hard, as though it's a sea inside me, with tides. A new heart made of devouring. I keep having this urge to stick my hand in it, straight down, just to see what will happen.

I keep resisting that urge. So far.

June 14? Not that it matters

Fuck

fuckfuckfuckfuckfuck

I'm so sorry, Zissi. I'm so so so very sorry.

I won't forgive myself.

Breathe in and out, Maureen. In and out. In and in and out and

[undated]

This will be the last time I write anything in here. Before I go, I will put this notebook somewhere in the building where another person will find it. I don't particularly care if anyone ever learns what became of me, but I think that Zissi's friends and family deserve to know what happened to her. And Zissi deserves an honest account of her … death? *Probably* her death. But I hope not. I cling to that hope.

Here's what happened:

I was lying on the floor in the heat, because the linoleum is cooler than my mattress, watching the paint slowly peel off the walls, marinating in my own stink. It was late afternoon, and the light was gold across my skin, across the milk crate bookshelves and the folded keyboard in its corner. The light was gold everywhere except where it fell into the hole in my chest and became nothing, became dark. I guess I was watching that, too. Then there was a knock on my door. A short, sharp knock, deliberate and unmistakable.

I figured it was my downstairs neighbor, the one who thinks I make too much noise. I ignored it. It came again, and again.

"Go away!" I shouted.

"Maureen?" someone cried through the wood of the door, and I knew Zissi's voice immediately. I remembered that Virginia Fur had a show coming up, and that if I hadn't missed it entirely by now, I'd definitely missed a lot of important practice and prep. All those texts I hadn't answered suddenly unfurled themselves in my mind. Everything about life outside my barren little apartment seemed so distant and trivial, some moderately interesting daytime TV show I'd once watched while home sick as a child. Even though I knew it had only been a handful of days since the hole began to be a problem. Less than a week.

I figured Zissi had come on behalf of the band to tell me off for flaking, and I felt a little bit bad for her—for all of them—but mostly I felt bad for myself. I still remembered Zissi's face the last time I'd seen her, the disgusted way she'd looked at my bloodstained shirt. ~~What shapes would her face make if she laid eyes on me now?~~

"Fuck off, Zissi!" I yelled. "I don't want to see anyone! Tell Cyra she can forget about me! I'm out of the band!"

"Maureen!" Zissi yelled, pounding on the door. "We're all worried about you! What the hell is going on?"

I hoisted myself off the floor and walked over to the door. Holding my chest well away from it, I pressed my face and hands against its heavy, smooth dead-tree surface. It smelled of dust and sweat and old beer, or maybe that was me.

"Zissi," I said, as kindly as I could, not wanting to shout anymore. "It's none of your business. Please, for both our sakes, just leave now."

"At least open your door, Maureen. Tell me that face to face."

"No," I said. "How did you know where I lived? And how did you get in?"

"Your brother's name is Dylan, right? He used to work with my girlfriend at the frame shop. I asked him. And the front door of your building was ajar, lucky me."

I considered asking whether she meant girl-friend-as-in-friend-who-is-a-girl or girlfriend-as-in-roman-tic-partner, then dismissed the question. It didn't matter. ~~I ignored a sudden flutter in my gut, a twisting lurch.~~ "Zissi, I'm sorry, but I can't see anyone."

"Maureen, I only want to talk for five seconds. Let me see that you're not sick or ... hurt. Then, I promise, I'll go. It's not my business if you want to self-sabotage."

~~My intestines were a rollercoastering tangle.~~ "What if I *am* sick, Zissi?" I asked her. "What if I *am* sick or hurt? What if I'm sick or hurt in a way that no one can do anything to help?"

I could hear her breathing on the other side of the door. She drew a long gulp of air into her lungs. "Then at least let me see it for myself, Maureen. At least let me understand what's going on. I care about you, you know."

"Not really," I admitted. "I mean, I don't think I knew for sure that you cared. Most people don't."

"But I do."

We both stood in silence for a moment, listening to each other breathe through the wood. Then I made the worst decision I've made in my entire life. God help me.

"Do you promise not to freak out?" I asked Zissi. "Do you promise not to be afraid of me, or ... repulsed?"

Another silence. Then she said yes, she did promise, and her voice was very small and grave. And so I took a deep breath, and I unlocked the door, and I opened it for her.

Zissi was wearing a dress that made her look like she was going to church. Her hair was soft and shiny, pushed back behind her ears. I felt even grimier than before. She frowned when she first glanced down at my naked chest, and then her wide eyes went wider. I saw disgust flicker across her face, and fear, and then something like awe, but finally her features settled in a configuration I couldn't quite identify. Pity? I think maybe it was pity.

She took a step forward, into my apartment, and I took a step back. "Oh, Maureen," she said, "what on Earth happened to you?"

"I don't know," I told her. I gestured helplessly at the hole. "At least you can see it, too. I guess that's good."

"*Good* ...?" Her voice broke off, incredulous. She took another step in my direction, reaching out. "Maureen, it's horrible. You poor thing. Did you do this to yourself? Oh my God."

"How could I do this to *myself*?" I demanded, as she took another step towards me. She began to reach out, and I lurched away from her again. "Why would I *want* to do this to myself?"

"We can bandage it up," Zissi was saying. "We can get you to an ER. They'll be able to help you ... Holy shit, Maureen. I think there's something moving in there."

I looked down at my chest, but I saw nothing moving inside the hole. I saw nothing. Darkness, blackness, empty space devoid of light. I started to tell Zissi I didn't know what she was talking about, but I stumbled on an empty can I'd left on the floor and I tripped. ~~I tripped, that's all, I swear that's all, I'm sorry.~~ And as I started to fall backwards, I thrust my body forward to try and get my balance again. I instinctively grabbed hold of the closest solid thing I could, which was Zissi.

I grabbed Zissi. I pulled myself up using her body. I could smell the clean mint of her mouth as she gasped in surprise and horror. Our breasts touched.

And then, before I had time to push her away, before she had time to scream, it got her.

The hole pulled her inside itself with the same ruthless appetite it had shown for tape measures and beer cans and me.

She was, of course, too big to fit, so it crumpled her up like flesh origami. There wasn't much blood, but there was a crunching, grinding sound as her skin and bones and meat shifted and stretched and compacted. I heard screaming, then, but I realized soon enough that it was my own. Zissi never made another sound, after that one little gasp. Perhaps she was dead in an instant, or hypnotized beyond feeling, beyond hurting. Perhaps it only *looked* painful. I hope so. I really, really fucking hope so.

When it was over, I was on my back on the floor again, shuddering and howling and crying. The downstairs neighbor banged on his ceiling, but that only made me louder.

The golden light had turned to dusky indigo and then to a sickly streetlamp glow before I calmed down enough to sit up and take stock of the situation.

Zissi was gone without a trace, and the hole had expanded tremendously.

It takes up most of my torso now, from collarbone to navel. It's grown out of its circular shape; the inflamed edges are the edges of my body. From the front, my chest is a silhouette of a woman, a girl-shaped blot of dark. When I reach around to touch my back, it's still there, skin and spine intact. The hole leads not through me, but directly into something beyond me. Unless it simply crushes everything it eats down to an invisibly tiny point, I suppose. But maybe it's a portal. Maybe it's a tunnel to some otherworld filled with giant moths and singing and beer can U.F.Os. Maybe Zissi is there now, in the belly of the beast, shaking the void out of her skirt.

Soon enough, I'll find out. The tug of the hole is stronger. I feel it lapping at the inflamed skin surrounding that numb space, converting more and more dirty, sweaty flesh into not-me. It makes it so difficult to move, to lift and carry objects. I have to hold this book and pen at arm's length across the kitchen table. (Forgive my sloppy handwriting.) When I'm done, I'll sneak it downstairs. Leave it in the laundry room, maybe, atop a coin-operated machine. Someone will find it before long.

And when I've done that, when I've left my record, I'll ouroboros myself. I'll stick my hands straight down into the dark and see where the suction takes me.

That's the only way this can end, whatever this is. Whatever it will turn out to have been in the end. I wonder if I'll get to know, somewhere deep in that infinite mystery. Even when I imagine the only thing waiting for me is oblivion, I feel a surge of relief thinking about it. It would be a pleasure to stop existing. A long-standing itch I finally get to scratch. There's no reason to hold off now. ~~I've done irreparable harm, and Zissi will never, never come back.~~

My only fear is this: what if I put my hands in the hole and nothing happens at all?

Therianthrope

Even a man who's pure at heart and says his prayers by night, they say. And you aren't a man. And you were raised an atheist. And you've never been pure of heart. Your heart is a dark, hateful engine. It fuels your four padded feet as they tear down the sidewalk after the screaming woman. Tiffany. Sandy hair, fashionably layered. Suit jacket. Gold jewelry. It's not yet 6 p.m., but you can see the moon in the daylight sky. Passersby gawk at you and scramble for cover and hold up their phones to take videos, but no one tries to help Tiffany.

Her ankles wobble. It must be hard to run in those heels. You tense your hindquarters and spring as she tumbles to the concrete floor of the world. You can smell her fear, cold and sour, spiced by a faint, piquant note of subconscious arousal.

You've never felt so much like yourself.

When you were a baby, you never stopped crying. You couldn't sleep. You were born with a canine tooth already grown in and a head already thatched with black hair. As you grew, you remained a fretful insomniac. Your other teeth came in early and they came in sharp. Your father, who was a dentist, was proud. Your mother, who was not a dentist, was worried. She gave you a baby doll to play with: an expensive one the size of a real baby, with soft skin and a pursed mouth with a hole that you were supposed to pour water into. The doll even had a diaper to change.

"I always wanted something like this when I was a little girl," your mother said, smiling at you expectantly.

You held the doll by one leg, making her open-and-shut eyelids flutter. She had a pleasant texture, squishy yet firm. Your mouth itched as you smiled back, but you knew enough to wait for your mother to leave before biting down on the doll's leg. Chewing her to a pulp was heaven. You worked your way slowly up her body for two weeks, then shoved her spit-soaked remains in a box under your bed. You told your mother she was lost. Your mother seemed to buy it, but she never gave you a doll again.

A little later, when you were not quite five, you had an accident. At a neighborhood barbecue, you tried to play with a stranger's nervous husky. You growled at him, grabbed his ears ungently. That was the kind of goblin child you were.

You don't remember the moment he attacked, but you remember the shock of blood, the smell of spit and animal fear up close, your breath and the dog's breath entwined as though you had always been connected by teeth and pain and terror, and always would be. You remember a wet, loud sensation that filled you up and drowned all your usual thoughts and feelings.

You couldn't tell if you were screaming or not, but you must have been, because you heard running feet and adult voices and then you heard thuds and scared yelps and the dog wasn't on you anymore; you felt the absence of his weight as almost a loss, and your vision was a haze of red.

Then you were in the hospital, and your head felt huge and numb, and you couldn't see out of your right eye. Your mother was holding your hand. She wouldn't look at you, but she gripped your fingers so hard they started to go as numb as your face.

Miraculously, there was very little permanent scarring. You were under the impression for many years that the dog had eaten your eye, but you found out as a teenager it had to be surgically removed when you were in the hospital. Punctured and lacerated, infected, rotting inside your head. You have no memory of this. A mental image that has persisted in your daydreams and nightmares for twenty years is of dog teeth fitting themselves around the jelly of your eyeball. You imagine the dog's furred throat moving as it swallows your sight, taking your perspective into itself.

You never hated dogs. You understood the husky. An eyeball would be more satisfying to bite than any doll's plastic flesh.

———◇———

It was difficult adjusting to the loss of your stereoscopic vision, but by the middle of elementary school you couldn't remember what it was like to have it. You didn't mind your glass eye. You minded the way other kids gawked at you and teased you and ostracized you. Maybe that wasn't really because of the eye. Maybe the eye was just a convenient excuse.

Maybe it was because they sensed something wicked growing inside you. You sensed it, too. It lay in the cage of your ribs like a bristling animal. It sent thick black filaments running through your muscles, making them twitch; you felt the filaments brushing against the back of your skin at night and you knew that one day soon they'd erupt into fur. You dreamed of fangs and claws and the cold wash of moonlight. You woke up sweating and itching between your legs, your lengthening limbs askew. You thought you should feel horror and revulsion. Instead, you couldn't wait for the wickedness to reveal itself.

It didn't.

Puberty dusted you with new hair, true, but mostly it just betrayed you. You grew tall, but not tall enough. You stayed thin, but not thin enough; your breasts and hips grew until you were shaped like a violin. You hated the way they swayed as you moved. You hated the way they made people look at you, the things they made people say. Someone was always calling you a *beautiful young woman*.

You let your leg, armpit, and pubic hair grow out. You cut the hair on your head short and spiky. It didn't stop the comments. You wanted to die.

Every month, blood spilled from your body. You liked to sniff it furtively in a bathroom stall between classes. Sometimes you wet a finger in the blood. Put the finger in your mouth. The thin bright red tasted different than the clotted dark.

In middle and high school you were still ostracized by your female classmates, but boys started asking you out. You found them boring and unattractive. They were only interested in your body, and in such a timid, tepid way you couldn't even get decent sex out of them. Your first kiss was in seventh grade. Jason F. ran away after you bit his lip hard. You lost your virginity in tenth grade. Steve K. flipped out when he realized you were on your period. You removed your glass eye and threw it at him, and that was the end of that. *Psycho bitch. I'm telling everyone what a psycho bitch you are.*

When you were seventeen, you started going to bars with a fake ID. The ID wasn't that convincing, but you looked a lot older than you were. You drank the bitterest drinks you could find. You made bartenders prepare obscure cocktails you found online, showing them the recipes on your phone. You danced, sometimes, when the alcohol was fizzing through you in a numbing, joyful wave of forgetfulness.

One night, a man found you dancing. He was the most handsome man you'd ever seen. Gold stud in one ear. Beard nearly blue. Big eyes, big ears, big teeth. His body wasn't bigger than yours, but it felt bigger. Because he was handsome, and smiling at you, and because you were drunk, you ground against him for half an hour and then let him take you home. He said his name was John when he first introduced himself. He said it was

Frank when you were leaving the bar. You let it slide; God, he made you wet.

JohnFrank fucked you hard and everywhere but his bed. He ran a kitchen knife against the inside of your thigh. He tied you at the wrists and ankles with extension cords. He gripped you tight around the throat and squeezed until you saw flowers bloom in your good eye, then disintegrate into burnt-edged holes. He said he was going to kill you, and you could tell from his voice and the shine of his eyes and teeth in the dark that he meant it. You grinned and laughed soundlessly.

His grip relaxed a little.

"God," you croaked. "Don't stop. What are you waiting for?"

His hands left your neck. "What's wrong with you?"

"Nothing," you breathed. "This is the most incredible thing that's ever happened to me. I really want you to do it." Your voice was so scratchy you barely sounded human.

JohnFrank flipped you over and began to untie you. "Well, that takes the fun out of things," he said petulantly.

"Chicken," you said, but the word got lost in a cough.

He sent you home, and that was the end of it. You looked and waited for him at the bar where you'd met, scanning the crowds each Saturday night in excitement and dread, but you never saw JohnFrank again.

———✦———

You left your parents' place at twenty. With your dad's money, you secured a small apartment. You stayed in the city where you'd grown up; it didn't seem worthwhile to move. Everywhere a person like you could go was more or less the same, anyway. You worked retail, then graduated to low-level office jobs. You kept to yourself during the day. At night, you kept going to the bars. Not every night. Maybe three or four times a month. You'd leave around midnight with the best-looking man, or the most violent-looking man, who'd have you. You'd try and convince him to knock you around a little. Some of them kicked you out, or got an Uber home in a hurry. Some of them responded with enthusiasm—beat you, raped you, robbed you.

It wasn't enough. It didn't satisfy. But it was something. You lived for those sparkling, drunken nights of danger. The wickedness inside you stayed trapped, pacing its cage of bone, howling at the moon behind your false eye and your true one. During the day, it slept. And the days were gray and flat and endlessly, frictionlessly boring.

Until you met Tiffany.

She'd been the receptionist at your office for a while. Weeks, maybe months. You didn't notice her until she got into the elevator with you one evening. Instead of ignoring you and avoiding eye contact, she smiled. Asked if you had weekend plans.

"Not really," you said. "Why?" You didn't bother to keep the hostility out of your voice. Tiffany was your age, about your height and build, but she might as well have belonged to a different species. Her makeup was like something you'd see on a magazine cover; you could barely tell she was wearing it at all. She looked perfect. She wore a slightly old-fashioned skirt suit and matching shoes. There were gold stars in her ears and around her throat. You could smell her laundry detergent, or maybe her perfume, or her soap. Lavender and mint.

"I was just wondering if you wanted to come out with me and the rest of the girls on Saturday night." Her voice was like her scent. Soft, soothing. "You always keep to yourself. I thought you must be lonely."

The rest of the girls. Never in a million years. "I don't think I'm up for a crowd."

"Oh." Small ditch dug between her impeccably groomed eyebrows. "Well, would you like to meet up for a drink tonight, then? Just us? I'm not busy." She seemed so sincere.

You were going to say no. What could someone like Tiffany want with someone like you? The elevator chimed and the door swooshed open. Her smile was lovely.

"Sure," you told Tiffany's pseudo-silk back. "Just tell me where."

———◇———

You'd been to the Barcade before, but for Tiffany, you pretended you hadn't. The gimmick was all in the name: a bar and a nostalgic arcade, like the kind people ten or twenty years older than you might have haunted as adolescents. There were game machines. Neon lights and tinny, electronic blip-bloops. An incongruous soundtrack of modern pop hits. Carpet like the upholstery covering bus seats. Even a singing animatronic cat lady with big, furry breasts in a black crop top with the Barcade's logo on the front. Tiffany grimaced at her as you walked past on your way to a booth.

"That thing is so gross," she said. "Only part of this place I don't like. I wish they'd get rid of it; not all their customers are college boys."

"I don't mind," you reassured her. "This is all really neat—thanks for showing it to me. What're the best cocktails here?" You slid into red pleather benches, facing each other.

"They do pretty good G & Ts. Usually I just have a couple beers."

You don't like beer, so you ordered a gin and tonic. You ordered four more gin and tonics as you sat and talked and watched the neon rainbows dance across Tiffany's face. Her skin was so smooth. You wanted to touch it. If you were a man, you'd touch it, you thought. If you were a man, you would bring Tiffany home with you and ask her what she wanted you to do and do it all until she was satisfied, until she couldn't stand it anymore, until she came again and again into your mouth and your hands.

The conversation started awkward and slow, but as you both got tipsy it became fluid, funny. Devoid of much meaningful content: you joked about work, let Tiffany share all her office gossip. But you'd have talked about dryer lint to watch Tiffany's mouth move under those shifting lights. She would have made dryer lint seem interesting. Words swam up from her throat like shining bubbles. You laughed, and she looked startled.

"I'm serious, though. Joel from accounting, he's totally bald. I mean, *totally*. No eyebrows, no eyelashes, no anything. It's some kind of disease. He has a really good wig and, like, these fake eyebrows and eyelashes and sideburns he glues on every day. Sheila swears up and down it's true. She even showed me a picture of him where one of the eyebrows was slipping off." She grinned. "It was sort of diving towards his ear, like a little worm."

You laughed again. "That's nothing," you said. You tapped your glass eye. "I'm a cyclops." And you told the whole story of the husky, the accident, the operation you don't remember. With gin fuzzing up your brain, you couldn't tell how Tiffany was taking it. Her face rippled before you. Slick pink lips, eyes the color of a swimming pool. No, a spring leaf. No. Something else.

Suddenly her hand slid over yours. Just for a moment, but it felt like it had burned you, like the imprint of her palm would be branded on your knuckles forever. "I'm so sorry that happened to you," she said. "No wonder you're ... well, the way you are. But really, you shouldn't feel insecure about it. Nobody can tell! You look normal. You look pretty."

Your heart swelled; your heart fell. Tiffany didn't understand. But she was trying; she wanted to. You pinched the back of your hand where she'd touched it. Did you want another drink? You couldn't decide.

"It's not about how I look. It's about who I am. It's about what's under my skin."

Tiffany frowned and asked what you meant. She called over a man wearing a tight Barcade T-shirt and ordered another Corona Light. You ordered a Blue Hawaii to mix things up a little. Before it even arrived, you were spilling words across the table. You told her about the man who first choked you, how he was going to kill you.

Tiffany's eyes glistened. She shook her head. Her hand hovered over yours, but did not touch it. "I'm sorry," she said again. "Oh my god, that's incredibly fucked up. I'm so sorry. Listen, there are hotlines you can call if you need to talk to someone about—"

"You still don't understand!" Your interruption was louder than you meant it to be, and you were standing, bristling. You could feel the fur scratching below the surface of your back, trying to break through. People at other tables stared, startled. The waiter arrived with your drinks and you sat back down quickly.

"You don't understand," you said again. "I wanted it. I needed it." You sipped your Blue Hawaii through its long plastic straw, and the night broke apart.

You were laughing and Tiffany was crying. You hugged her and she swayed into you. You were both apologizing for something.

Now you were playing a Beetlejuice-themed pinball game. Losing. The lights and bells shrieked until you couldn't think.

Tiffany stood guard outside the bathroom as you retched into the toilet again and again. There was blood in what came up.

In the parking lot waiting for a ride. Asphalt under you, white-gold stars up above, a grinning moon. You lifted your skirt and pushed aside your underwear and pissed on the ground. The smell was acrid and comforting in its familiarity. Tiffany was making a face at you. Tiffany kept looking at you and then looking at her phone. You kept looking at her and then looking at the moon.

You had your head on her shoulder in the car. A woman was singing about loneliness over a spacy electronic soundscape.

You were at home in your bed and Tiffany wasn't beside you. *Good*. You wanted to have something more special with her. You wanted to be sober the first time. You wanted some sort of tenderness.

For the first time you could remember, you spent the rest of the weekend alone in your apartment and happy.

You had forgotten to exchange numbers with Tiffany, so you couldn't text her, but you found her Instagram. You spent hours scrolling through the photos in a shaft of sun. Tiffany with a puppy, with a gaggle of friends, with her mother and grandmother, in a canoe on a lake. Always laughing, starry, summer-eyed.

You didn't have an Instagram account. You thought about making one, just to message her. You kept chickening out, unfolding from your lazy circle on the armchair, pacing the dusty floor, coming back to your phone. There would be time. You'd see her at work soon enough.

When you dreamed, you dreamed she was with you. You gently bit the silky, peach-fuzzed skin around her navel until it mottled and bruised. She flipped you on your back and straddled your chest, her fair hair and pointy, pink-tipped breasts swaying above you. Her hands found your throat and squeezed, and squeezed, until you felt something start to rise. It was coming through your nostrils, your ears, your eye sockets. It was fur, smoke, a sound like the wind at night. You oozed out of your body in the shape of a great black dog, and you took her between your teeth.

In your sleep, your mouth twitched itself into something like a smile.

———◦———

On Monday, the other receptionist sat behind Tiffany's desk. Lacey or Lindsay or Lily, her name was. She was buck-toothed and dour, with long fake fingernail claws you half-envied.

"Out sick," Lacey-Lindsay-Lily told you, when you asked. *Hungover*, you surmised she meant. You hoped Tiffany would be all right tomorrow. On your lunch break, you bought three blood-red roses in a glass jar.

"Can you make sure Tiffany gets these?" you asked Lacey-Lindsay-Lily.

"Sure." She tapped her claws on the desk. "You wanna leave your name? A card or something?"

You nodded. Asked to borrow some printer paper, scribbled a quick note on it. *Had a great time on Friday! I've never met anyone like you before; can't wait to see you and talk again! Hope you're feeling better. xoxo*

This morning, Tiffany was back at her usual place. Finally. You'd started to get really worried; maybe she was sick after all.

When you walked into the office, she beckoned you over. You practically ran.

"I can't accept these." Her voice trembled as she shoved the jar of roses at you. They were wilted; it had been a couple days.

"Why not? It was nothing, I promise. I wanted to give you something."

"I just can't. I'm sorry; it's too weird."

"Do you want to grab lunch together? I've missed you."

"I can't today."

You leaned towards her. She looked pale and tired. "After work, then. Please? We don't have to actually go anywhere. We can just sit on that bench outside the library and catch up for a couple minutes."

She sighed. "Yeah. Okay. Fine." Her voice was stronger now. "That's all right."

Even with the return of the roses, you felt light and full of optimism. You barely ate, barely paid attention to your work, barely noticed the way your co-workers kept giving you sidelong glances and whispering behind their hands. Your blank, bare cube made the roses seem cheerful although their heads had started to crust and curl at the edges. They still smelled alive.

You hummed to yourself as you typed. You were still humming when you left the building. Crossed the road. Walked a block down to the public library where, as promised, Tiffany was waiting on the broad metal bench, picking at its peeling paint. She started, wild-eyed, when you sat down beside her.

"Shit! I didn't see you come up."

"Sorry," you said. "How're you doing? How's your dog? I saw on Instagram he was having tummy problems."

She moved away from you, down the bench. "Don't look at my fucking Instagram!" she snapped. Then, before you had time to react to that unexpected outburst, in a calmer voice: "Listen, don't take this the wrong way, but I don't want to see you again outside of work. I don't think we should be friends. And I'm straight. I don't want to get flowers from other women."

"But. I." Your head whirled. This wasn't anything you'd been expecting. Your feelings tumbled and clashed. It was difficult to form words. "*You're* the one who asked me to go out with you. You're the one who asked in the first place. I thought we had fun." You sounded so plaintive; you hated that.

"I felt sorry for you," said Tiffany. Still calm; condescending, even. "I really did. I was trying to be nice. I thought you were just shy, see, even though everyone else thinks you're weird and stuck up and aloof. Figured I might bring you out of your shell a little."

"And it worked! Look, I swear I didn't mean to make you uncomfortable by coming on to you. We can just be friends. I'm not even really a lesbian, honest. I'll never buy you roses again." You might as well have been on your hands and knees, prostrate.

"That's not the point!" Tiffany snapped again. She must have hated your whining and begging as much as you did. "It worked, but you know—some people ought to stay inside their shells! I can't handle being friends with you!"

"What do you mean? Tell me what you mean!" You moved towards her on the bench, pushing her back until she was cornered against one of its curlicue armrests. You could smell her toothpaste. You could see a glimmer of fear in her face. You liked it.

She shoved you aside and sprang to her feet. Her hands were fists, her cheeks flushed. "I mean that you're a freak. You're a fucking nutcase! You need professional help! You're a drunk and you're sexually confused and you have these absolutely demented fantasies and you don't know how to tell when you're making other people feel scared and uncomfortable! Or maybe you just don't *care*!"

It certainly wasn't the first time you'd heard any of this. For some reason, though, it all felt new. Each truth was a glass knife plunged between your ribs and pulled downward, razing your heart and your breath and your very bones. You were coming apart. You were dying. You wanted to be dead. You wanted to have never existed at all. The thing that hid inside you un-coiled itself. It pressed hard against the back of your skin—more knives, or pins and needles, each one forcing itself through a pore.

You fell forward onto the sidewalk, scraping your palms. A pressure was building in your skull. Blood began to drip slowly from your nose and mouth. It seemed too bright.

Tiffany was saying your name. She sounded concerned. It might have been enough, but she was still backing away, moving farther from you, her hands hovering in front of her chest. A defensive posture, protecting her vital organs.

You erupted from your old body, skin and clothes shredding across new muscle and wet pelt. Your glass eye popped from your face like a cork from a bottle, and you realized you could see depth again. Two eyes, new eyes. Only, the colors were different.

You stood on all fours, your tail alert, your ears full of sounds and your snout full of scent. Hunger prodded you to give chase as Tiffany screamed and began to run, heels clacking, hair flying. It was easier to get the hang of your new shape than you would have thought, before. You were not thinking now. You are not thinking. Only moving in pursuit, moving on instinct, finally unfettered.

You bite Tiffany's neck. You hold her down with your mas-sive paws while you bite out her right eye and swallow it like a piece of candy. There are gunshots. Some commotion. It doesn't matter. Still alive, Tiffany sobs underneath you. She's trying to say something with her smeared red mouth. That doesn't matter, either.

Behind you, beside the shabby library bench, the remains of what you were ripple in the breeze like ribbons in a little girl's hair.

Leavings

Chantal's hands hovered over the stinking thing on the bed-sheets. It was long and wet-looking, the color of clay.

"Never seen a turd before?" snorted Meggy. She snapped a pair of latex gloves over her own hands, which were fat and leathery. "Gotta get used to some gross shit in this line of work, kiddo. Literally *and* figuratively."

Meggy scooped up the turd and carried it into the bathroom. She set it in the toilet bowl and flushed. "There. All gone. Strip the sheets, Chantal."

"Should we do anything special with them? Put them in a bag separate from the rest of the linens?"

"This ain't the Hilton, sweetie." Meggy chuckled. "We use strong bleach. It'll be fine."

Chantal dutifully stripped the hotel bed of sheets and pillowcases. She worked them all into a neat bundle and dumped everything in the laundry bag on the side of the housekeeping cart. She took fresh linens from the cart's bottom shelf and re-made the bed. She tried to breathe only through her mouth;

the smell of the turd still hung in the air. It was an odor like rotting leaves and bad teeth.

"Good," said Meggy, watching. "Nice hospital corners. You'll be ready to strike out on your own tomorrow, I think. Gonna tell Andrea that."

"Really?" It was stupid, Chantal knew, to feel a flush of pride and excitement. This was a terrible job. Still. You had to take your dopamine rushes where you could get them.

"Really." Meggy smiled. "Why don't you show me just how fast you can do the rest of this room by yourself?" She planted her hands on her broad hips, leaned forward a little, and groaned. "My back's killing me. I'm gonna sneak out for a smoke real quick, then start on 9B."

"Sure."

Meggy left, rubbing the small of her back through her worn polyester uniform. Chantal began dousing the bathroom in pastel pink and blue spray cleaners. Their harsh chemical stench battled the lingering ghost of the turd for supremacy.

Chantal was a lot more efficient at cleaning than she'd been a week before, when she'd started working at the Kingdom Immanent Deluxe Motor Inn. But she had nothing on Meggy, who had to be at least sixty and who had, as she'd told Chantal several times, been employed as a housekeeper since she was Chantal's age.

Meggy was vacuuming room 9B's threadbare carpet when Chantal caught up with her. She winced every time she had to bend her back a certain way. "You got the keys?" she asked.

Chantal nodded.

"Go on to 10B. Make yourself useful." Meggy's abundant but ill-cared-for gray curls were starting to straggle out of their bun and hairnet. They swayed over her bloodshot eyes.

Chantal pushed the cart forward so it sat between the doors of 9B and 10B. Across the central courtyard from her, someone was leaning on the paint-flaking iron railing that surrounded the motel's second-story walkway. They were watching Chantal. She squinted, but she couldn't make out their face; whoever it was wore a broad-brimmed, elegant hat, like something out of an old movie. Incongruously, they had on a black tracksuit and black knitted gloves, even though it was summer.

Chantal decided the best course of action was to ignore the strange figure. Kingdom Immanent attracted some real shady types.

She knocked on the door to 10B and loudly said, "House-keeping!" She waited a moment. When no one responded, she unlocked the door. She glanced back across the walkway, but the black-clad person was gone.

10B was about as neat as the rooms ever were. The bedsheets were rumpled and the window was slightly open. The TV remote lay facedown on the floor. The air smelled faintly like copper, or rust. No tip left on the nightstand, unfortunately, but easy work.

Chantal went into the bathroom. Off-white tile, no towels disturbed. The toilet paper still folded into a neat triangle at the end of the roll, like the guest hadn't even had to take a dump.

Chantal's eyes wandered to the bathtub. It was full of some-thing. Bloody and soft, folded and twisted around on itself so many times Chantal couldn't determine its proper shape.

It reminded Chantal of a buck she'd once seen in the middle of shedding his antler velvet. Bone-branches red and clotted with gore; flesh-shreds dripping off their prongs like mottled, moldy ribbons. Skin peeling around the base of the antlers and flopping down over the deer's narrow, beautiful face.

There was much too much *something* for it to be antler velvet, unless deer could grow big as houses.

Chantal decided to fetch Meggy. There had to be something she was missing, some fact that would render the soft, bloodied mound mundane. Meggy would know.

"Well, I'll be damned," said Meggy as she looked inside the bathtub.

"Have you ever seen anything like it?" asked Chantal.

"Nope," said Meggy. She sounded more intrigued than dis-gusted. With a hearty grunt, she squatted beside the tub and reached inside to touch the thing with her bare hands. "It's warm," Meggy announced.

Chantal shuddered. Meggy's hand was smeared with san-guineous red.

"You know what this reminds me of?" Meggy continued to poke and prod. She didn't look at Chantal.

"Antler velvet?"

"Ha! No. It reminds me of these old folktales my dad used to read me when I was a little girl. Years and years and years before you was a twinkle in your parents' eyes, of course. Some of them were about these people that could change shape by taking off their skin and putting on a different one. They'd have to hide the skin they weren't wearing, leave it someplace safe while they did their business so nobody'd steal it."

"That sounds morbid."

"It wasn't really," said Meggy.

"But those are just stories," Chantal pressed. "Someone could have been hurt here, right? We should *do* something. What should we do?" The rust smell seemed to get stronger and heavier by the second. Chantal was sure it came from the tub. She felt lightheaded.

"Get out of here," said Meggy. Her voice wasn't unkind. "Go and fetch Andrea from her office. I'll stay."

Chantal didn't run, but she did walk very quickly, swinging her arms and taking big, emphatic breaths. She didn't burst through the door to Andrea Cordello's closet-like lair, but she did push it open without knocking.

"Something's in the bathroom of 10B," Chantal started.

Ms. Cordello looked up from a pile of paperwork with an irritated expression.

"There's a lot of blood," said Chantal, hating the discrepancy between what she'd actually seen and the small, flat words coming out of her mouth. "There's like ... part of an animal, maybe. You'd better come and see. Meggy's up there now."

"A dead animal?" Ms. Cordello frowned as she stood up.

"Something like that, ma'am."

"Lead the way," said Ms. Cordello, and Chantal did.

The door to 10B still stood open a little. Ms. Cordello began to step inside, then froze. She withdrew her foot from the doorway and stood once more on the concrete walk.

Chantal peered over her supervisor's shoulder. Meggy was nowhere in sight. The room was steamy, as though someone had just taken a long, hot shower.

A plump, pretty young woman sat naked on the bed. Her long hair covered everything indecent, and she didn't seem embarrassed by the other women's presence in the least. Chantal felt her face flush with shame.

"It's all right!" said the woman. Her curls spread out on the bed around her thighs. "Is there something I can do to help you?"

Ms. Cordello gently closed the door. "I was informed the occupant of this room was out," she called through it. "One of the housekeepers reported a dead animal in your bathroom. I'm sorry to ask, but—would you know anything about it?"

"No," said the pretty woman. "*I'm* sorry." A muffled, musical laugh. "Believe me, I'd be the first to complain if that was the case. There's nothing in the bathroom except soap and steam. You can come in and look if you want; I'll put on a towel."

"No, no," said Ms. Cordello. "There must have been some mistake. We're sorry to bother you. I'll send a housekeeper by again later to service your room. Unless, of course, you'd prefer not to be disturbed."

"I swear—" said Chantal. Her head spun. "Look," she began again, desperately, "I'll try the rooms next door. I know what I saw. Meggy saw it, too. She's around here somewhere, waiting."

"Make it quick," said Ms. Cordello. "Don't waste my time."

———✦———

9B was immaculate, devoid of velvet gore and Meggy alike. 11B was trashed and filthy, with nothing in the tub but a wet mat of hair escaping into or out of the drain. Meggy wasn't in there, either.

Chantal wasn't really surprised by Meggy's absence. She *was* surprised when Ms. Cordello didn't fire her on the spot, or even chew her out much.

"Don't come to my office with nonsense like this again," she told Chantal. "Now, I'll ask you once more: do you know where Meggy went?"

"I don't know. Honest to God, I don't."

"She'd better not have quit," Ms. Cordello said, more to herself than to Chantal.

"I don't think she would—not like this. Not Meggy. But you never know. I promised I wouldn't lose any more girls this year. I can't afford—" She broke off and ran a hand through her sensible bob. "Chantal!"

Chantal's spine straightened. "Yes, ma'am?"

"You'll be good on your own for the rest of today, right? You can handle what's left of the second floor?"

"I think so, ma'am."

"Excellent," Ms. Cordello said. "Then you get back to your work, and I'll get back to mine."

Through the door to 10B, Chantal heard a voice singing words she couldn't make out. It sounded sort of underwatery, or like the singer's mouth was full of something wet. Yet the tone was high and clear. She shivered for no good reason. The air was very warm and starting to get humid as the day advanced.

When Chantal had almost finished up in 11B (where, despite or because of the immense mess, she pocketed a $5.75 tip), she heard the distinct sound of the door to 10B opening, then closing. She heard footsteps moving away. It sounded like two people walking together.

Chantal stuck her head through the door of 11B just in time to see the couple's backs descending the stairs. There was the pretty woman, now wearing a satin dress that was (in Chantal's opinion) much too tight for her. Her wide hips and ass swayed and wriggled under her veil of hair. She was arm in arm with the figure in black Chantal had seen earlier. The person still wore their hat and gloves; Chantal could see no sliver of bare flesh poking out anywhere.

"Meggy?" Chantal called.

Neither of them stopped or turned around.

Soon, she heard a car start in the parking lot. Then she heard it drive away.

It was still light when Chantal got off work. That was the nice thing about summer. At the bus stop, she looked up at the sunset. She looked out at the road. She looked down at her sneakers, which had a crusty, reddish-brown material stuck conspicuously to their laces.

She hadn't noticed that before. Maybe it was shit. Maybe it was dried blood. Maybe it was just dirt.

Chantal sucked the end of her cigarette and decided against making a closer investigation.

Eventually the bus came to take her away, and she put out her cigarette and got on.

The Witch's Wife

I.

When the Witch's wife was alive, she was a tall woman with hair the color of perfect ripe corn and eyes the color of perfect ripe corn fungus. She would laugh when the Witch told her this, and her laugh was like the sound of cheerful crows descending to feast on a cornfield's crop.

"Corn fungus, Elaine?" she'd say. "Why not gray like stones, or gray like the sky before a storm, or gray like the fur of a cat?"

"I think fungus is very beautiful," the Witch would say. Her name was not Elaine. She'd given up her name long ago, when she first became the Witch. Still, her wife had to call her something, and her wife was adamant that professional titles did not suffice between lovers and spouses.

"I'm sure you do," the Witch's wife would say as she traced the thick webwork of raised scar tissue that criss-crossed the Witch's thighs. "You have a unique sensibility, Elaine. I like that about you."

When she was alive, the Witch's wife had long, slim hands with articulate fingers. She kept her nails very short and her cuticles neat. Everything she did with her hands, the Witch thought, looked like sex, or magic. Not the Witch's magic, not true magic, which is harsh and bloody and often desperate, but the magic of men in top hats and women in spangles who pull scarves, knives, rabbits out of thin air. The Witch would watch her wife paring an apple, or dexterously assembling a kitchen table from a kit, and she would want her more than she wanted to keep breathing.

When she was alive, the Witch's wife drove an old car with a trunk that had trouble staying closed. She sometimes had to tie it shut with a length of bungee cord. The Witch offered to replace the car many times, but the Witch's wife always declined. "I'm sure that would be a lot of effort for you," she'd say. "Don't cause yourself pain over a car. I'm good with Christopher. We've been together since I was in college, and he still runs fine."

The Witch's wife had named her car Christopher. The Witch's wife had a thing about names, and the Witch never understood it. For the Witch, names were unnecessary more often than not. Besides, names were powerful. You didn't just go around naming things to be cute. You didn't just go around handing out your name to anyone who asked for it. Unless you were the Witch's wife, who had business cards. The business cards said her name on them in swirling letters, and then *Freelance Illustration, Traditional and Digital Media* in smaller, plainer letters under that.

When she was alive, the Witch's wife's name was Laura Charmian Zell. (She never used the Charmian, except on those business cards.)

Now the Witch's wife is dead, and her name isn't anything anymore.

It wouldn't feel right for the Witch to call what's lying on the worktable in front of her "Laura."

The Witch looks at the corpse of her wife. It no longer has eyes the color of corn fungus, or very much hair the color of corn. Christopher the car was destroyed in the accident, crumpled and crushed and mangled. The Witch's wife fared only a little better. If the Witch were going to give her wife a funeral, it'd have to be closed casket for sure. Not even the best mortuary makeup artist could undo the damage done to the body of the Witch's wife.

The Witch is better than a mortuary makeup artist. The Witch is better than a doctor or an EMT. The Witch is a Witch. When a Witch wants something enough, the usual laws of the universe bow respectfully and get the hell out of her way.

"Well, then," says the Witch to her Familiar, which trembles in a corner of the garage, "let's get to it." She snaps latex gloves onto her hands and selects the box cutter from her tool tray.

II.

The Witch first learned she had an unusual power quite young, and by accident.

The child-who-was-not-yet-the-Witch wanted many things. She wanted them with an intensity that made her feel constantly sick inside, as though her stomach were filled with poison flames. She wanted to be beautiful, like her older sister had once been, so that their mother would love her. She wanted her sister's bone disease to disappear and leave Emily healthy, running and smiling again, hugging their mother, defending the Witch-child from their mother's constant criticism. Beautiful, untouchable.

She wanted to have at least one friend, or, failing that, to frighten the other children at school so much that they no longer teased her. Or laughed at her. Or shoved her face into the dirt during recess.

She wanted to be smart enough to understand everything the teacher told the class right away. She wanted to stop struggling with reading and writing. She wanted to unlock all the secrets of the world.

She wanted to have power over everything that hurt.

One day, the wanting inside her grew so intolerable that she punched a wall with her small fist. It was a flimsy wall, and she hit it as hard as she possibly could. Her hand made a crater in the plaster.

Her hand was lacerated and sore, stinging and bloody around the knuckles. But what really made her mad was the damage to the wall, which had been smooth and unblemished. She'd had an effect, but it was a tiny effect, and all it did was break the world a little bit worse. Furious, the child took her fist from the pit she'd made and struck herself full in the face as hard as she could. As hard as she'd hit the wall.

For a moment, she thought she'd half blinded herself. Roses of pain blossomed across her vision. Her left eye felt like a hole in her head. When she closed her right eye, the world was dim and blurred, all indistinct shadows. She was barely conscious that she was crying until she felt snot and tears start to run down her philtrum and into her mouth.

Her sight settled back to normal, although her eye still hurt. (Later, she'd glance in a mirror and see she had a big purple shiner.) She blinked. She blinked again. She registered what she saw in front of her and blinked a third time to make sure she was seeing it right.

The crater she'd punched in the wall was completely gone. The plaster and paint were smooth. She could not even tell where it had been.

And when she returned to her homework, she found that the letters did not sway and swarm and rearrange themselves in front of her eyes, but stayed pinned in place so she could decipher them, although it was still slow going.

And the next day at school, all the other children stayed far away from her. They whispered behind their hands when they saw her coming, and scattered like cockroaches when she passed by.

Though not book-smart, the child was quick on the uptake in some things.

She hit herself, and her mind grew clearer as her skin clouded with bruises.

She pulled out her eyelashes with her mother's tweezers, and two of the toughest, coolest boys invited her to play pirates with them at recess.

She slammed her fingers in the car door on purpose, breaking two of them. Emily came downstairs for breakfast the next day, smiling and saying she felt a little bit better. Emily read the classified ads in a silly voice; she ate a bowl of oatmeal and kept it down. Emily braided her little sister's hair and exclaimed over her little sister's bandaged hand.

The child burned the soles of her feet with matches. This did not make her beautiful, as she had wished, but she began to carry herself differently. Her eyes were bright. Her face looked proud and secretive. Her steps were swift and sure, and her gaze was unnerving even to adults. She was beginning to learn what she could do.

Of course, she was still only a child. She wasn't quite canny enough to completely hide the damage she inflicted on herself. Her mother rebuked her clumsiness, ridiculed her appearance, and returned to fussing over Emily. That wasn't so bad. But various grown-ups at school and church started to get concerned. They asked her gentle, probing questions she never knew how to answer. There was talk of calling Child Protective Services.

One grown-up who noticed the changes in the child belonged neither to the staff of the public elementary school, nor to the Methodist church. In fact, this particular grown-up barely left her house at all. And her house happened to be right next door to the house where the child lived with her mother and sister.

Her mail (junk, bills, and dirty magazines) was addressed to Ms. Nadia Horvath. The other grown-ups called her a shut-in, an invalid, or crazy. The kids just called her a Witch.

III.

Laura was an artist. She was other things on occasion, too, especially before she was the Witch's wife: a barista, a pizza delivery driver, a janitor at a middle school. But she was always an artist. She drew pictures. They were elaborate, layered creations, tapestries of the dreamland in her skull.

Before she met the Witch, Laura's drawings had dark colors and often featured stillness, bones, ruins, fossils. Lone figures striding through beautiful wastelands, or drowning in seas filled with flowers but no fish.

After she met the Witch, Laura's drawings became brighter and more psychedelic. They contained far more people and living animals, although these people and animals tended to be sprawling, shambling, ripped open with ecstatic expressions on their faces, melting into one another. The seas were filled with flowers and fish alike, and with things that were flowers and fish at the same time. Laura was commissioned less often, and she sold much less of her original work. It didn't matter to her. She was happy with her newer pieces, and the Witch saw to it that she wanted for nothing.

"I wish I could do what you do," the Witch would some-times say, watching Laura create dragons and comets and rat kings from lines of pencil on paper, from lines of digital stylus on tablet. "My drawing ability never progressed beyond stick people."

"Well," Laura would respond, smiling, "I can't do magic. If I cut myself, all that happens is I bleed on the furniture. So we're even."

"What you do *is* magic," the Witch would say, wrapping her arms around her wife's shoulders.

"That's very sweet, but it's bullshit," Laura would reply. "I can't fix anything by drawing about it. I can't paint money out of the ether. I can't create new life with a picture." Then she might look pointedly towards the Witch's Familiar, which might be curled sleeping on a corner of the sofa, or might be awake and snuffling around the perimeter of the room.

The Witch made her Familiar out of her own breasts. She never liked the breasts while they were still attached to her body, and it was the final straw when one morning, showering, she discovered a lump the size of a small bird's egg between her armpit and her left areola. She cut off both tits that afternoon, using the pain to transform their combined mass into an inde-pendent animal. The Familiar looked something like a cephalo-pod on land. It had large, long-lashed red eyes and no mouth; it didn't need to eat. It did, however, have a gently pulsating slit in its forehead that the Witch assumed was a sort of sensory organ.

"Mmmm," the Witch would say, considering her Familiar and pressing her face into Laura's corn-colored hair. "You could help me create life, if you wanted."

"Someday, Elaine," Laura would say, momentarily abandoning her work, reaching up to pet the top of the Witch's head. "We'll have a child. I'm just not quite ready yet. There's plenty of time."

"Of course," the Witch would agree. Her powers had limits. She could never predict the future. "There's plenty of time for that."

IV.

The Witch pants and sweats, sitting cross-legged on the tarp on the floor of the garage. Her body is slicked mouth to thighs with blood: bright red, dark red, and drying brown-black. She knows how to heal herself quickly, how to protect herself from infection, delirium, and mortal damage by means both medical and magical. She is still shaky and exhausted, lightheaded as an overeager sprinter. Her tools lie in a neat row beside her. She must rest for a while before she even thinks of continuing. The garage stinks of rust and formaldehyde.

The Witch's wife is still on the table. She looks different than she did a few hours ago. Her skin is soft and smooth, unmarred and unbroken. Her hair spills golden from her head, tumbles in a waterfall down to the concrete at the edge of the tarp. If it weren't for her bloodless pallor, the sunken eyelids covering empty sockets, the strange little crater on one side of her head where part of her skull and brain remain missing, she might be asleep. But her heart is a still stone in her chest and her lungs don't breathe. The Witch's wife remains stubbornly dead, no matter how much of her body the Witch's magic restores.

The Witch pulls herself away. She drags herself back into the house. She peels off her gloves, her jeans, and her apron. She showers in ice-cold water, still thinking of her wife's corpse in the garage, willing the skull and brain and eyes to regrow, willing the lungs and heart to quicken, willing the mouth to speak again, the hands to work their own peculiar magic in the world. She slaps herself across the face. Once, twice, three times, as hard as she can. She does not cry. She isn't crying. The water running down her face comes from the shower head. Witches don't cry.

The Witch leaves the shower. She re-dresses in a pair of sweat-pants and one of Laura's T-shirts, a shirt that still smells like Laura used to smell. She slouches at the kitchen counter and holds her head in her hands. Her Familiar trundles across the tile carrying a glass of tap water in one of its tentacles, a roast beef sandwich in another. The Witch grunts her appreciation. She takes the glass of water and downs it in one long swallow. Next she tears into the sandwich. Drippings run down her chin and plop on the surface of the counter, on her sweatpants, on the floor. Laura would have cared about the mess. The Witch doesn't give a damn.

"I think I need to try something new," she says to the Familiar.

The Familiar blinks its long lashes. It looks concerned.

"No, I will *not* accept my limits," snaps the Witch, who understands her Familiar's mind. "If I accepted my limits, I would never have become a Witch in the first place."

The Familiar makes a faint whistling sound. It cocks its head and undulates a few tentacles.

"Fuck you," says the Witch. "It's much too late for that now. I'll love her until there's nothing left of me but dirt."

V.

"Hey!" hissed Ms. Horvath from the edge of her yard one morning, leaning over the picket fence between her house and the Witch-child's. "Bruisy girl! Come here."

The child-who-was-on-her-way-to-becoming-the-Witch had been walking to school, but she was in no hurry. She looked curiously at Ms. Horvath. "I thought you were an agoraphobe," she told the woman. "That's what my mom says, anyway."

Ms. Horvath snorted. She was wearing a fuzzy bathrobe and plastic clogs. Her shoulder-length hair was frizzy and colorless. Her eyes were a washed-out brown. She looked haggard but normal: not tall, not short, not thin, not fat, not dark, not pale, not young, not old, not pretty, not ugly. The only strange things about her appearance were the thin scars branching up from beneath the collar of her bathrobe, and her missing right hand. On the stump of her wrist, she wore a plastic and metal contraption like a lobster's pincer.

"What happened to your hand?" asked the child, at the same moment Ms. Horvath said, "For pity's sake, girl, I don't have a *phobia*."

They stared at each other. The child stifled a nervous laugh. Ms. Horvath glared.

"I'm perfectly capable of leaving my house," she continued. "Most of the time, however, I prefer not to. As for what happened to my hand, I'll tell you that story if you tell me why you're always walking around looking all beat up."

The child looked warily down at the ground, then up at the sky. "I don't know if I should," she mumbled.

"Well, tell me or don't. I think I can help you, that's all. I think we might have something in common." Ms. Horvath raised her eyebrows.

The child's eyes narrowed as she looked directly at her neighbor. "My mom would never, ever hit me," she said, "and I'm not having trouble with bullies, if that's what you want to know." She shuffled her sneakers on the sidewalk. "I'm not hurting myself because I'm sad, either, or because I want to punish myself for something I think I did wrong, or so other people will feel sorry for me the way they feel sorry for my sister. The guidance counselor already asked me about that, and Pastor MacReady, too."

"I see," said Ms. Horvath, stroking a fencepost with her lobster pincer. "Why do you do it?" Her robe slipped open a little so that more of her scars were visible. They grew thicker around her collarbones, rippled down into the valley between her breasts. A robin sang from somewhere in Ms. Horvath's overgrown garden.

"When I ... when I hurt myself, if I wish really hard at the same time as I'm doing the hurting, my wishes come true." The child's face felt hot. It sounded so stupid when she said it out loud. "The things I want to happen end up happening. Or, at least, they'll happen a little bit." Emily wasn't getting worse, but she wasn't getting well, either. Their mother still didn't seem to love her younger daughter very much.

Ms. Horvath smiled with long yellow teeth. "That's called magic, kid. You've got a natural talent for it."

"Magic?"

"Sure. You could be one hell of a Witch someday, if you wanted."

"You're not supposed to say 'hell'. And witches aren't real. They're only in stories, like ghosts or vampires."

"Do I look like I'm in a story?" Ms. Horvath spread her arms wide in a look-at-me gesture. Her bathrobe suddenly seemed a sorcerer's garment. Her eyes flashed. The garden behind her looked darker, more sinister, filled with brambles and riotous vines. Something scuttled out of the bushes. It resembled a huge spider, but it only had five legs, and they were thicker than spider legs should be. Each was tipped with a dark-lacquered claw.

The child trembled, but she took a step forward. She pushed open the fence gate, which was unlatched.

"If you're in a story," she said, "then I guess I'm in a story, too."

"What an excellent answer," said Ms. Horvath, who looked like her ordinary self again. She scooped the spider-creature up with her hand that wasn't a lobster pincer. The child noticed that the spider-creature interlaced itself with her fingers perfectly, like it was clinging to its mirror image.

"Come into my parlor," Ms. Horvath continued, turning back towards her house, not checking to see whether the child was following, "and I'll tell you about all kinds of important things. I've been wanting an apprentice."

———◇———

The Witch's Apprentice was a diligent student. She told her mother that Ms. Horvath was tutoring her after school and on weekends in exchange for help with household chores, and in the strictest sense, this was not a lie. But instead of writing or mathematics, Ms. Horvath taught her the rules of magic.

The main rule was this: All magic is powered by loss and by pain. The Witch's Apprentice had intuited as much for herself, but Ms. Horvath laid it out more precisely. Yes, she acknowledged, some Witches would try to work magic using the loss and pain of others rather than giving up anything, inflicting any pain upon themselves. Some Witches were child-thieves, animal-torturers, cannibals, murderers, and so forth. However, Ms. Horvath was of the opinion that these methods were likely to fail, or even backfire on the Witches who used them.

"You can't cheat magic," she told her Apprentice as she showed the girl how to clean and bandage a deep cut. "Just like you can't cheat gravity. Moreso, in fact! I'm sure you could magic your way into levitation if you were determined, though it'd require a heavier price than anyone ought to pay for a party trick. But magic knows, girl. It knows if your sacrifice doesn't really grieve you, if your desire is insincere. It knows if you're trying to get something for nothing, or make some other poor sap pay the price you owe. As a wise man once said, a true Witch must be willing to rip out her own liver for what she wants, and not expect to get it back."

"It doesn't always have to be flesh, though," the Witch's Apprentice observed. "I gave up my name."

"And it was a pretty name, the only thing you had that was prettier than your big sister's, isn't that right? You cried when it was gone."

"I did." The Witch's Apprentice smiled slightly. "I liked my name. It's funny; I don't remember what it was anymore."

"Pain," said Ms. Horvath, lighting one of her fat cigarettes that smelled like resin and skunk. "Pain and loss. They're not only physical. Not always." Her handle Familiar clambered up the back of her perpetual bathrobe to perch on her shoulder.

"It's always worth it," said the Witch's Apprentice. "Isn't it? There'd be pain and loss anyway. When I look at my scars, I can think 'there, that's something I did. I chose to make that mark, for a good reason.' Nobody else decides when I get hurt."

Ms. Horvath blew a smoke ring. The Witch's Apprentice kicked her legs back and forth in her chair, watching the white gauze around her wrist bloom slowly red.

"But you know," said the Witch's Apprentice, "there's another reason I do magic."

"Oh yeah?" Ms. Horvath blew a second smoke ring through the dispersing remnant of the first.

"I want my mom to love me. I want to protect people I care about. I want Emily to get better, all the way better, forever."

"Oh, child." Ms. Horvath laughed, but it wasn't a laugh that sounded like she really thought anything was funny. "Those are crappy reasons to do magic. Best you forget them as soon as you can."

"No. Why should I?"

"Magic can do a lot, but it does have limits. You can't always make people love you. You can't protect others from all the harm the world will deal them."

"That's lame," grumbled the Witch's Apprentice. "That's not what I signed up for, and I don't like it."

"You didn't sign a damn thing. You were born with a power and you chose to use it. But listen: You don't need to care about other people so much. Treat them kindly, sure, if it floats your boat. But learn to master your feelings before they master you. Love can be another kind of trap, girl. Another way the world sneaks its ropes around you and takes away that free will you hold so dear, that ability to decide when and how it is that you get hurt." Ms. Horvath stroked her Familiar's bony back. "We

Witches are solitary, you'll discover. We learn to love our own company, and we don't need anyone else's. That's the way it is and the way it ought to be. Someday, your mother and your sister will be gone from your life. Someday I'll be gone from your life, too. And someday, you'll wake up and look around and find you don't miss any of us one jot."

VI.

The Witch is back in the garage. The Witch's wife is still dead, still lying on the table. The Witch's wife's eye sockets are still empty. The Witch thinks of two irises the perfect color of corn fungus, gone forever now. The Witch's own eyes are the color of mud. They blink rapidly, squinting, wet. The Witch is gathering her courage for what she is about to do.

"You know," she remarks to her Familiar, "I've never actually removed a body part before, except when I made you." She holds a clean scalpel tight in her gloved right hand. "But Laura will need to see," she continues. "Laura is an artist. She can't draw if she can't see." The Familiar makes a soft, worried sound.

"Besides," says the Witch, taking a deep breath, "I need to sacrifice something big. Pain alone won't be enough. It never was for Emily."

VII.

Seasons passed, and passed again. The Witch's Apprentice grew in skill and power and knowledge. She grew taller and more scarred. She spent more and more time with Ms. Horvath.

School, and the other children there, interested her less and less. She grew to prefer her own company. She had nothing to prove to anyone else. None of them could touch her. Their opinions didn't matter.

The Witch's Apprentice cut and burned and fractured herself, and Emily's health waxed and waned. But Emily's periods of respite from illness became shorter and shorter, less and less pronounced, even as the Witch's Apprentice's magic became stronger. The Witch's Apprentice no longer had much time for her sister, even when Emily was relatively well. The Witch's Apprentice kept her head shaved, so she had no hair to braid. The sisters stopped watching TV together. Still, they cared for each other. The Witch's Apprentice made flowers grow all around Emily's hospital bed, poppies and orchids in the middle of January. Emily still got sicker. She seemed to become smaller and younger, receding into herself as the Witch's Apprentice grew towards the sun.

The girls' mother spent more and more time in her bedroom with the lights out and the blinds shuttered. Drinking. Weeping. Asleep. The Witch's Apprentice found she no longer cared much what her mother did.

The Witch's Apprentice was the one looking after the family now. She was the one with the means and ability. Her mother stopped going to work after a while. The Witch's Apprentice learned to bleed on leaves and turn them into ten and twenty and fifty dollar bills. She learned how to play the stock market. They were fine. Her mother never asked her where the money came from, and neither did Emily—although by that point, Emily was so ill that she rarely said anything at all.

When Emily finally died, the Witch's Apprentice wasn't surprised. A worm of guilt gnawed at the base of her brain.

"Maybe I didn't want her to get well badly enough," she told Ms. Horvath at Emily's funeral. She'd been surprised that Ms. Horvath was willing to leave her house for the occasion, and wise enough not to mention it. Ms. Horvath avowed that she was interested in her Apprentice's progress, but that she had no particular investment in the girl or her family. All the same, she stood with the Witch's Apprentice by the graveside as the narrow white coffin was lowered into the earth.

"Oh, kid," said Ms. Horvath, sighing as she tentatively laid her pincer hand on her Apprentice's shoulder, "of course you didn't."

The Witch's Apprentice pulled away, glaring at her.

"No, listen," said Ms. Horvath. "Think about how badly you'd need to want your sister to live, in order to halt this kind of disease. You wouldn't just need to hurt. You'd need to sacrifice something *enormous*. Would you give up your own life so Emily could have one? Would you give up your mind? Your heart? Your body? I don't think you would. You'll never, ever value another person that much, God willing. It's not bad to eschew martyrdom. It's not bad to want to live for yourself."

The Witch's Apprentice wasn't crying. Witches and their Apprentices never cried. But her words sounded fat and quivery as she spit them out. "I should've done *something* bigger, though. I could have."

"No," said Ms. Horvath. "It isn't your fault. You didn't make her sick. You didn't kill her. Shhh. Shhh."

"You told me someday she'd be gone," whispered the Witch's Apprentice. "You told me I wouldn't miss her."

"Eventually you won't. You might not believe it now, but it's true."

"I hope so," said the Witch's Apprentice. People were throwing shovelfuls of sandy dirt on top of the casket. The sun boiled the sky blank and pale. The Witch's Apprentice squeezed her eyes shut until they stung. She bit her lips until her mouth prickled with blood.

The next year, the Witch's Apprentice's mother died of a heart attack. Ms. Horvath became her guardian. The Witch's Apprentice was never sure if it was a legal guardianship or not. Whatever the case, no one turned up to give them any trouble about the matter.

The Witch's Apprentice slept on a futon in Ms. Horvath's TV room for the next few years. The Witch's Apprentice decorated the space with posters of bands she liked and broken pieces of dolls dangling from the ceiling on fishing line. Her books and clothes piled up in drifts on the floor. The TV itself was relocated to Ms. Horvath's kitchen. Still, Ms. Horvath never called the room where her Apprentice slept anything besides "the TV room."

"Don't get too comfortable," she admonished. "The minute you turn eighteen, you're out of here."

But it wasn't the Witch's Apprentice who left. On the morning of her eighteenth birthday, she awoke to find that Ms. Horvath and her Familiar had vanished as though erased from the house, lifted through the roof by aliens or God. Ms. Horvath's rarely used shit-colored Celica was still in the driveway. Half a joint smoldered in a shell-shaped ashtray on the kitchen table. When the Witch's Apprentice dared go into Ms. Horvath's bedroom, even her bathrobe was still there, lying in a heap on the carpet like a shed skin.

The Witch's Apprentice knew in an instant, down to the marrow of her bones, that Ms. Horvath was gone for good. Her apprenticeship was finished. She slipped the bathrobe over her own shoulders, where it hung awkwardly. She shut her eyes and waited for her sadness to stop.

VIII.

Laura lies on the table, cold and still. The Witch lies on the tarp-covered concrete floor beside the table, shaking, damp with sweat and blood. Laura has one left eye, sightless and glazed in her smooth, slack face. The Witch has one right eye, squinting and blinking through a haze of pain. The Witch's Familiar circles restlessly, nudging them both with its appendages.

"That didn't work either," mumbles the Witch. "It still wasn't enough. Fuck."

Her breath is harsh and halting. In, out. In, out.

"Ms. Horvath lied," she says to her Familiar after a little while. "Or maybe I'm just weak. I never stopped missing anybody. It's been twenty years, and I still think about Emily every goddamn day. I sold all Ms. Horvath's old crap in the end, didn't keep a single ashtray, and I still see things that remind me of her all the time. Things she would've disapproved of, mostly." The Witch manages a faint smirk. "She wouldn't have approved of Laura. Doesn't matter. They'll never meet."

The Witch concentrates on her breathing for a few moments more. Liquid runs down her face from her right eye, from the socket-wound that once held her left. "Familiar," she says, "I even miss my fucking mother. It doesn't stop. As long as I remember them, they're stuck inside my head. What good is magic, if ..."

The Witch doesn't finish her sentence. She struggles into an upright position. She gets to her feet. Her Familiar blinks with moist, anxious crimson eyes.

The Witch tentatively pokes at the one remaining site of visible damage on her wife's body, apart from the empty right eye socket: that dip in the side of her skull. The place where Laura's head was crushed, where something vital remains missing.

The Witch withdraws her hand and brushes her fingertips across her own temple. "My love and my grief have a physical location," she muses. "I can feel where they're writhing around in there, if I try. It's all just patterns in the meat."

The Familiar indicates its dismay.

"No," says the Witch. "I know what I have to do."

The Familiar pulls at the Witch's bloodstained pant leg with several tentacles at once. She shakes it off. "It'll be all right," she says, "no matter what happens. If it doesn't work, I still won't remember to grieve anymore. I'll be better off." She goes to her tools. She finds the bonesaw, the icepick, the scalpel.

"I choose this," she whispers as she examines her reflection in the smudged standing mirror beside her worktable, looking for the easiest way through her skull to the parts she seeks.

———

Laura didn't eat meat, but she liked the scent of blood, the copper and iron tang that always stuck to the Witch's skin. Laura was four years older than the Witch, but people always thought she was younger. Laura had dated men before she met the Witch, and most of them had been very cruel to her. Her past didn't seem to get Laura down; she was always laughing that laugh like a flock of crows. She liked to put her long pink tongue in the Witch's ear, between the Witch's buttocks in bed. Laura had a few friends she went to bars with on weekends, friends the Witch did not begrudge her but never bothered to get to know. Laura didn't speak to her parents, who lived in one of those big square states out West. Laura had bad breath in the mornings and pale stretch marks on her hips. Laura's body odor smelled like wet moss and one of her back teeth was silver. Laura had never been to see the ocean, and she was always asking the Witch to come drive with her there, come take a road trip, come, we'll camp on the beach, Atlantic or Pacific, they're both far away, it doesn't matter.

"Next summer," the Witch always told her. "We'll do it next summer."

———

The skin parts easily. The bone, slick with blood, is harder. It makes a peculiar sound specific to opening bone as the Witch grinds away at it. The pain grows along with the wound, receding to a profound but dull ache once her skull has transformed into a box with a hinge. Her brain nestles inside it like a bloated pearl. Still, this is easier than cutting open Laura's corpse. Having to do that, the Witch thinks, almost killed *her*.

She goes in with the smaller tools. Her brain is clay-textured and nerveless. There's no sensation as she clips out the parts she needs. Only a sense of lightness and absence, small pink and gray weights lifted from the burden of the Witch's self.

Her Familiar guides her shaking hands, keeps the morsels of flesh on the right track to their new home. The Witch can barely remember what she's doing anymore but she does it anyway, pupil blown wide, entranced. When she finishes, she mumbles the words for knitting bone back together. For fusing skin. A new, vivid scar encircles her shaved scalp. Laura's skin shuts itself, the crater now filled.

When she's finally finished, the Witch collapses on the gore-stained tarp. It smears her cheek like a bed of crushed strawberries. Her eye rolls back in its orbit, leaving only white jelly and bloodshot veins to meet her Familiar's worried gaze.

The Witch sleeps for a long, long time.

IX.

The Witch stands looking down at a one-eyed, naked woman on the worktable in her garage. The woman is dead. No, not dead. Asleep. The Witch can see the woman's chest moving slightly, up and down, up and down.

The Witch doesn't know how this woman came to be in her garage. She doesn't know why her head hurts so much, like it's been pierced with a hundred needles, like parts of her brain have been scooped out. She doesn't know why she can't see out of her left eye.

The sleeping woman's skull is a perfect curve. Faint blue veins pulse at her temples, just below a pink scar at her hairline.

Perhaps, the Witch thinks, one of her spells went wrong. She feels something like irritation or anxiety gnawing at her chest. It seems terribly important that this other woman awakens, though she isn't sure why.

"Hey," says the Witch brusquely, shaking the woman's shoulder. "Hey, you. Whoever you are. Get up already. Get up and get out of my damn garage." She waits. The woman shifts a little and sighs in her sleep. She mutters a word that sounds like "lane."

"Hey." The Witch shakes her again.

"Elaine?" repeats the woman, opening her eye at last. It is an eye the color of graveyard dirt, very bloodshot.

"Who?" asks the Witch, wondering why her heart has begun to beat faster.

———◦———

"Speaking of livers," the unicorn said, "real magic can never be made by offering up someone else's liver. You must tear out your own, and not expect to get it back. The true witches know that."

A few grains of sand rustled down Mommy Fortuna's cheek as she stared at the unicorn. All witches weep like that.

— *The Last Unicorn*, Peter S. Beagle

Close Encounter

When we walked into the clearing, an alien was there. It was covered in translucent goop like raspberry jam. Not covered the way a body might be covered in blood, we thought, but covered the way a body might be covered in clothes, even though we surmised that the alien was extruding the goop from somewhere inside itself, under the leaf-green skin.

My brother stepped up and introduced himself, offering his hand in friendship. Len was always very forthright, blunt, unafraid no matter the circumstances.

The alien stood there, staring at my brother as if in apology. It blinked its large, liquid-black eyes slowly. It had hair: what looked like a fuchsia Party City wig, tangled and ornamented with splintered twigs. Behind the alien we could see a camping tent, spotless yellow nylon except for the seeping blotches of raspberry jam goop around the open flap. Maybe a person had transformed in there. Someone ordinary, like us, a hiker carrying a canteen of water, a pack of hot dogs, a cooler of beer, a Swiss Army knife, extra underwear.

"Hey there, stranger," said Len.

We were both hoping for a transcendent connection, a miracle moment of E.T. contact.

Then goop oozed out of the alien's eyes, ears, and mouth, out from between its legs. The alien leaked like a filled donut squeezed hard in the middle. Its face was impossible to read.

Translucent, glistening red covered up all the green. It formed mounds at the alien's bare, four-toed feet. The alien knelt in the long grass. It retched and spasmed. More raspberry jam burst forth in a great splatter.

Some of it hit Len smack on his forehead. He shrieked and windmilled backwards into me. I lost my balance and dropped my backpack, all the gear attached to the backpack. I landed on my ass in the mud. A smell like fried, heavily spiced pork filled the clearing. Drool welled like a new spring in my mouth.

As I grabbed Len, I took one last glance at the alien. Its skin looked deflated. The Party City wig had fallen onto its shoulder. I could no longer make out the shape of its head. One black eye stared at us—mournfully?—through a wet gel haze. The pork smell was definitely coming from the jam stuff, and I put thoughts of shoveling it into my mouth barehanded firmly aside. I would not be disgusting.

Len and I ran back down the mountain. He clutched that spot on his forehead the whole way, rubbing it and moaning as he stumbled on the trail. "It has a taste," he kept saying. "I feel it in my sinuses. I feel it in my mouth. Some capsaicin shit." His tongue seemed thicker, his voice blurrier every time he repeated the words.

"Hold on," I said. "We're gonna get back to the car and I'm gonna drive you to the hospital."

Acid sloshed in my stomach; I felt scared and hungry at the same time.

———◇———

"We've been seeing a lot of this lately," said the ER nurse as she shined a light into each of Len's eyes. "An alien up in the woods, huh? They must be spreading."

"Spreading from where?"

"Out in the western part of the state." The raspberry jam had left a burn on the side of Len's head. She dabbed at it with a gauze pad of alcohol. "They're such a nuisance. Your brother's gonna be fine." She stepped back from the examination table. "We get that mess off your skin, you go on home, you never come back. Healthy as horses. Same every time."

"Thanks," said Len. His voice was flat and dazed.

"Just hang tight here. Dr. Carpenter will be in to look at you in a minute. I'm going to check your insurance." The nurse squeaked away on thick rubber soles and scarred linoleum tile.

Len lay back. "I feel very strange, Joey. Were there always aliens? Do you remember ever hearing about them before? Is this normal?"

"I don't know." I scratched up and down my arms through the sleeves of my sweatshirt. I felt phantom lumps of jam writhing slimily against my biceps. I knew they weren't real. I imagined them squeezing themselves into hair-thin worms and diving down the manholes of my pores. I scratched harder.

Dr. Carpenter came in and smiled at us with a lot of pale gray teeth. "I heard you boys had a run-in with our local aliens!" He snapped a pair of plastic gloves onto his hands. "This is a formality, really. You're fine. You won't even need antibiotics."

Len seemed on the verge of falling asleep as Dr. Carpenter commenced prodding him in all the same places the nurse had, and then some. Len's eyes dulled and his mouth hung slightly open. I wondered if his tongue was numb from the capsaicin shit. I wondered if the rest of him was numb, and if it had come on all at once. Maybe it progressed in pieces: the tongue, a toe, an ear. Navel, asshole, knee. Len's pupils were dilated, and I imagined them spreading out to cover the iris and white entirely.

I was careful not to touch him on the way back to the car, in the car, at home. For the first time in many, many years, I wished we didn't share a bunk bed. But the apartment was small, a studio.

Len reached out and brushed my leg hair with his fingertips as I climbed up to the top bunk.

"Fuck off!" I shouted, vaulting myself onto the thin mattress.

"What'd I do?!"

"Your hand feels all sweaty."

"Sorry." I heard Len's sheets rustling as he rolled over on his side in a sulk. "I still don't feel well."

"Yeah?" I lay back. I stared at the popcorn ceiling, its surface the surface of some desolate alien planet. "Well, the doctor said you were okay."

"Right." Was his voice clogged with phlegm? Tears? Something else?

"It's so weird that we've lived here almost our whole lives and never known about the aliens," I said. My voice sounded so reasonable I almost believed it myself. "But it really wasn't a big deal. We were so dumb, freaking out like that."

"Right."

"We'll wake up tomorrow and everything'll be normal. The same as before. We can pretend nothing ever happened." I closed my eyes. The alien planet disappeared.

Len didn't answer. I heard him breathing, though, in a quiet kind of wheezing, bubbling way.

I kept my eyes shut and made my own breath deep and even. If I pretended to be asleep long enough, eventually it would be true.

Everything was fine, and everything would be fine.

Strands of artificial silk-shiny hair the color of Hawaiian shirt hibiscus. Abandoned backpack. Beer cans rolling down the side of a hill, past the abandoned yellow tent. The smell of spicy pork. The saliva surging in my mouth. The peppery sting on my tongue. The dream of flesh torn open, deflated, spreading contagion, full of something shiny, amorphous, and brand new.

The Holy Incubus of West Virginia

I see him come down from the sky and land in the trees by the highway. I pull over right away. Quiet. No headlights; the pale of him is enough, under the full moon. Always knew this day would come. He's not an unusually large barn owl. Early on, I had a few false alarms with owls, before I understood how different from an owl he is. Though owls are very beautiful. His wings are feathered like an owl's, and noiseless the way an owl's are. His body is a human body, sort of—I call him "he" because everybody calls him "he," even though there's really no way to tell. I think he must be around my size, maybe 5'9", average build. Though the wings throw you off, they're so big. He could be a regular person, but with wings, except he's not wearing clothes and he's covered in all that white stuff. I don't think it's feathers, and I don't think it's hair, either.

I'm creeping closer through the bushes, scraping myself on blackberry thorns but making no sound. No sound, like an owl as it descends on its quarry. I'm trying to see him better. Maybe the white stuff is like that fuzz on moths, the fringe around the sides of their wings, whatever that's made of. Maybe that's why everybody calls him the name they do. I never liked the name, myself. Sounds too much like a D-tier Marvel Comics character. There's nothing cartoony about him. He's not like an insect. Maybe he's a man, and maybe he isn't. Maybe nobody except me knows how to recognize angels anymore.

There he is on the gravel of one of those rough roads through the woods nobody much uses. The highway almost doesn't exist from here. He's curved his wings so they surround him in a protective wall. He's crouched on the balls of his feet, under the moonlight coming down through the gaps in the pines, examining something he's picked up out of the forest dirt. The something shines in his fingers, whiter than he is, whiter than bleached bone or fresh milk. The shadow of the wings covers his face so I can't make it out. But his eyes flash as I step towards him on the road. They shine red like the light on top of a radio tower, signaling. All of a sudden, I know he knows I've been looking for him. Maybe it was his idea that I should look for him in the first place. He wants to be found. He's been waiting for years. Since long before he called out to me.

I take another step. I haven't thought enough about what I'm going to say. *Be not afraid. I come in peace. I mean you no harm. I'm only trying to know you.* Is that what I want to tell him, or is it something he's projecting into my mind, or is it both?

"Did you make the bridge collapse?"

Well. That's one way to break the ice.

His shadow-draped head shakes slowly. No.

"Were you trying to warn people about the bridge collapse?"
Another step closer.

He does kind of a nod and a shrug at the same time. Then
he stands up, letting whatever he was holding fall back on the
ground. Now I could see his face clear if I wanted, but something makes me look down. His muscles ripple beneath soft
moon-colored fuzz. His chest moves as he breathes. I want to
touch him. His wings spread wide. Their tips brush the bark of
the trees around the road. His arms spread wide. I don't dare
look at his face. You don't look at the face of an angel. But he's
calling me in. His arms are strong and smooth. I can feel his eyes
on me, stripping away my clothes, my flesh, my shame. He sees
everything, he sees it all. Down to the bloody core of what I am.
And he doesn't turn me away. I never thought he would, but
it's still a humbling experience.

My hands touch his pectorals. No nipples, so maybe he isn't
a mammal. I feel his heart. It's so fast. It feels like beating wings.
His wings moving to surround us both.

I take off my shirt as quickly as I can. My pants, my shoes.
They're unnecessary. The night air is soft and warm. My cock
is stiff. My cunt is wet. His body feels electric against mine, like
there's static between us, but it's not off-putting at all. I want
more.

He matches his palms to mine (no nails on his fingers, no
fingerprints), and clasps my hands tight. He pulls me to him
and grabs me by the hips with something lower down—another
pair of little arms. Inhuman fingers stroking inside the cleft of

my ass. I put my face into the velvet of his thick neck and close my eyes.

My feet leave the angular crunch of gravel. Dangling in air. A great, rushing wind.

We ascend.

Air beneath behind before me. Clutched to his chest. Pulling those fine strong filaments that glow moonbright. He smells only of summer air and pine needles. Fingers surrounding me, toes as long as fingers. I'm in his talons and I never want to be let go. I'm full of owl, I'm full of moth, I'm full of angel digits. We could go to the moon. He could eat me on the wing. I don't mind.

Radiolight scarlet pulse in my brain. He's got a message for me. It's important. He's got a warning. I've been chosen to receive, and I receive. Stretched wider than I thought possible. Above the branches, beneath the stars. Another bridge collapse inside me. I can't keep it in; don't let me go. His not-fur not-feathers all slick with me now. Dripping milk-blood-cum-sweat onto an earth I can't see. I'm trying to hold onto the message. I won't tell you what it is. Some things should stay between lovers. I write impending doom on the backs of my eyelids, to stay and burn there for the rest of my life, and I let him take me back down.

He pushes me gently towards the pile of my clothes. I don't want to part, but I understand, and I can't argue. It feels awkward and heavy to walk on the ground, supporting my own weight. The moon makes everything silver and blue as I struggle with my fly. I can still feel him watching me.

When I turn to him, he kneels. Scoops up that glittering thing from the gravel. Holds it out. Trembling, I take it. It chimes and sings as it leaves his wet, sticky fingers.

Once again, I won't tell you what it is.

Once again, some things should stay between lovers.

But I put it in my back pocket, and he nods at me. For just an instant, I forget not to look at his face. It is nothing like a man's face, or an owl's, or an insect's. I half-scream without meaning to. I fall into a supplicant's bow, bruising my knees and the flats of my hands. I smell summer air and pine needles and the slightly sour tang of my own orgasm.

And when I raise my nose from the road, he's gone again. I don't even see him in the sky, winging away. Just the stars and the moon and the shadows of the tree tops.

I head back to the car, because what else is gonna happen, really?

I'm driving home on the highway with my headlights casting their beams on the yellow line ahead. It's super late, so I'm alone in the dark. No other cars. No anybody out here. There's a strange emptiness that descends after you get something you've wanted for a long time. There's an object shining in my back pocket, there's an object poking into my ass as I shift in the cracked leather seat. I don't know what I'm going to do next, exactly. No one will believe any of this if I tell them. No one ever believes the important messages.

Well. Almost no one.

I did. I do. Otherwise I would never have come here.

I turn on the radio to keep from feeling lonely. It's all preachers and nighttime conspiracy theorists. Nothing of consequence. When I find a station that's just static, with occasional music seeping through, I keep it there. It's more honest. And the hours roll on, and eventually I sleep in my twin-size bed, my arms held out to either side off the mattress to dangle in empty space.

Desire in the Flooded World

when the waves march in like an army of froth, the moon is
the puppeteer, dragging along her feet, dirtying her jelly sandals.
wash up, madame, your knee is skinned. let us bandage it.

— Ivy Jones, "just the other day nina came to me asking how
big the moon is"

I.

In the flooded world, Kurtis Lacklin Jr. nurses the wounds
in his soul, which have begun to open up again. He has scurvy
of the mind and heart. He watches the permanent layer of dead
brown water on the floor of the basement rec room soak the
shins of his trousers. He would watch his toes prune and shrivel
in the murk, were it not opaque.

In other places the water has fish in it, fish that nibble tick-
lesome and hungry at exposed skin. The Lacklin family basement is abnormally toxic. It's because of acid or heavy metals or
something. Kurtis wonders how much poison he's absorbed in
eighteen years. He wonders if that's what's killing his father.

Kurtis Lacklin Sr. hasn't said he's dying, but it's pretty obvious. The vicious pustules and streaks of veiny red black that creep across his body. His weeping into the basement lake late at night, when he assumes his eldest son isn't watching and cannot hear.

There is a stack of papers set beside Kurtis on the ratty plaid couch. The papers are covered in neat block letters, written in black ink and blue ink and graphite pencil. The papers tell the story of Kurtis's love for Selwyn Kimball, who works at the 7-11 and is five years older than he is. Kurtis has been in love with Selwyn since Selwyn was thirteen, and a full-time girl. Thirteen-year-old Selwyn babysat for Kurtis and his younger siblings.

These days, Selwyn is only a part-time girl. When Selwyn works the cash register at the 7-11, Selwyn is a man. His black hair always looks damp and hangs over one eye like the wing of a crow sheltering an egg. You can't see the water stains on his black work pants. One of his canine teeth is silver. He remembers Kurtis, teases him about growing strong and handsome, doesn't see how Kurtis's heart throbs and bangs. He's still taller than Kurtis, who takes after his petite mother rather than his tall, heavyset father. Kurtis still has to tip up his chin to meet Selwyn's one-eyed, level stare, like a little boy.

The papers describe all this and more in a swarm of untrained adjectives. Often, the papers lapse into rhyming, haphazardly metered, erratically spaced poetry that Kurtis realizes is dreck. (*Selwyn, your tooth cuts through me like a dagger / I can't help*

*watching your hips when you swagger / through the puddles to get
to the beer / all I want is to hold you to my body so near.*)

Kurtis pretended the papers were a love confession to Selwyn
at first, but before long he had to admit to himself that they were
only ever for his own eyes. They were a diary, like something his
boy-crazy little sister might write. He'd never show this shit to
Selwyn Kimball, never. Selwyn would laugh at him. Or look at
him with pity and confusion, which would be worse.

Tonight, Kurtis has decided to try and put his secret love to
bed for good, or at the very least destroy the damning evidence
of it. What if his father found the papers, the poems? His mother? Nyleen?

Nyleen would never let him hear the end of it. His parents,
who haven't spoken of Selwyn in years, would be horrified.
Maybe they'd kick him out to make his own way in the damp
and the muck and the ceaseless rain.

Kurtis feels his heart like a deep cave carved through his flesh,
a scooped-out, lacerated pit. He's mildly surprised when he
looks down at his chest and sees only the dingy white fabric of
his shirt. His hands are shaking.

He takes a sheet of paper from the top of the pile. He takes a
lighter from his pocket and sets the corner of the page on fire.

When the flames have eaten almost up to his fingertips, Kurtis lets it go. The ashy remnants of the paper fall into the dark
water. Some float; most sink. Soon they're all invisible anyway.

Kurtis squeezes his eyes shut and takes a shuddering breath. He hopes no one upstairs will be wakened by the smell of smoke.

He grabs the second paper from the stack. Lights it up. Lets it fall.

II.

In the flooded world, Nyleen Lacklin pretends she's floating in outer space. The riverroad beneath her is the Milky Way; the spangled reflections of moonlight on the water are a million churning suns passing under her makeshift raft.

Nyleen didn't make the raft herself. Her oldest lover, Vincenzo, gave it to her. "So you'll always have a way to come to me," he'd said.

Nyleen uses the raft for nighttime visits not just to Vincenzo, but to all her other lovers: Owen, Peter, Karl, Sid. Unlike Vincenzo, they're around her age. Or only a few years older, anyway. Sid, Karl, and Owen still live with their parents, so she has to sneak around their houses, be as quiet as possible when she's jerking or sucking them off in childhood bedrooms full of anime posters and stuffed toy fish. Peter lives in the college dorms, which are kind of institutional and ugly and cramped, but cool for being some of the most watertight buildings in town. When Nyleen visits him, Peter puts an old gym sock over the outer doorknob so his roommate won't come in and disturb them.

But tonight is for Vincenzo. Nyleen's heart rushes ahead of her to meet him as she paddles the raft towards his bungalow at the edge of town. Nyleen's oar is something from a kayak or a canoe, with a long red-painted metal handle, while the raft is primarily made of an old oak door, marked by many superficial wounds but thick and glossy even after years of hard use. Her spaceship, Nyleen thinks. Who needs to pass a stupid driver's test in the flooded world? With this, she can go almost anywhere she cares to go.

The rain tonight is light, transparent, barely there. Nyleen doesn't feel it, but she imagines raindrops glittering in her hair like jewels. She smiles to herself as she paddles up to the bungalow and hitches her raft to the dock in front. The water is especially deep here. Vincenzo's house is a new one, built on stilts and concrete bolsters on top of the old, dry town's ruins. Nyleen closes her eyes and pictures beds and couches rotting underwater, minnows swimming in and out of picked-clean skulls.

"There you are," says Vincenzo from the doorway. "My little naiad."

Nyleen opens her eyes and rises to greet him. Heat already throbs between her legs.

Vincenzo is probably about as old as Nyleen's dad, and maybe even older, but Nyleen still thinks he's handsomer than any other man she's ever met in real life. He has the chiseled, sad face of a movie star from eighty years ago, with stark creases in his cheeks. His eyes are dark and deep-set; his still-thick hair is white streaked with black. His voice is the voice of a movie star from eighty years ago, too.

Vincenzo takes Nyleen's hand and pulls her into his arms. They kiss. Vincenzo is also a better kisser than Nyleen's other lovers. Probably because he's had more time to learn to do it right. He kisses with tenderness, then with vicious passion, with the exact right amount of moisture and tongue.

The only part of Vincenzo's kisses that Nyleen doesn't love is when she starts to pull away and he clutches her back to him, unwilling to let anything end on her terms. Nyleen never presses after the clutch, though; she doesn't want Vincenzo to look at her like she's some skittish little girl. That's what's great about Vincenzo, not just that he's a real adult, but that he treats Nyleen like *she's* a real adult, too. As long as she behaves like one. When Nyleen gets too petulant, or hesitant, or gloomy, or demanding, Vincenzo looks at her like he's the stern but caring master of an untrained lapdog, like Nyleen has chewed a hole in one of his best shoes.

Vincenzo leads Nyleen to the living room, and she waits on his brown velvet couch while he pours her a drink, as he usually does. Nyleen traces a little arrow-pierced heart in the velvet with her fingertip, then smooths it over before Vincenzo returns.

Vincenzo hands Nyleen her drink, which is blushing pink with a garish red cherry for a garnish. He sits beside her and sips the martini he's made for himself. Nyleen picks the cherry off the rim of her glass and sucks it lasciviously.

"Is your father still doing ... poorly?" asks Vincenzo.

Nyleen huffs. "I'd prefer not to talk about that. But, yes."

"And your mother? Your brothers? How do they fare?"

"They're fine. Same as always. Kurtis is a spineless sissy and Avery's a little freak, but they're sweet. Mom's pretty tuned out. I'm not sure she ever knows what's going on." Nyleen takes a long sip of her drink. It tastes like bubblegum and lighter fluid. She's long learned to relish the burn, and doesn't wince as the alcohol scours her throat. "I don't want to talk about them either, though."

"Of course, my dear." Vincenzo puts a hand on her thigh and squeezes it through her skirt. Nyleen turns her body towards him, trembling, anticipating his desire. Sometimes she thinks Vincenzo is the only person in the world who really loves her. His hands, still strong and smooth, are so different from her father's.

Nyleen imagines watching herself and Vincenzo from the outside, a hovering spirit. His tongue a darting eel in the cave of her mouth, his fingers diving beneath her skirt and into the cave between her legs. Nyleen's head spins pleasantly, and she tries to concentrate on the sensation, the sensation and the sexy picture the two of them make together, dignified older man and lush young woman. She tries to think of nothing else.

Outside the bungalow the raft bobs on the moonlit water, a door that will never be closed again.

III.

In the flooded world, Avery Lacklin wakes from an unfamiliar type of dream and finds that he's made a mess of his bedsheets. He sits up in a puddle of weak, rain-filtered morning light and swampy, sticky fluid. There's a fish smell everywhere. There's a salt smell like tears.

Avery's not embarrassed, but he is confused.

He's had sex ed in school, and his mother had a strained, stilted version of the Talk with him a couple years ago. And he's picked things up from listening to Nyleen and her friends. He knows what a wet dream is. But this doesn't seem normal. The stuff soaking the sheets isn't white but a shimmery brownish-green. There are little pearlescent bubbles floating in it, like frog or fish eggs. And there's so *much*—surely it's not normal, for there to be that much?

Avery reaches down and touches himself. He checks for new holes, for wounds. He gingerly feels his butt and his penis. The swampy stuff came out from inside his body. He's convinced of that. Without reason, beyond reason—he just knows it has to be his.

Once he's satisfied that he isn't injured, Avery stands up and strips the sheets from his bed. He wads them up into a dripping, smelly ball and shoves the ball inside his laundry basket. He runs to the bathroom he shares with his brother and sister, clad only in wet underpants, to take a shower.

But there, in the steamy cave behind the moldy plastic shower curtains, under the hot artificial rain, Avery notices more new things about his body. There are weird, fleshy webs creeping up between his fingers and toes. There's an itchy, grayish rash on his belly and thighs. Avery scratches it, and it flakes away in papery scales. Gross.

Avery scratches harder, and harder. He digs his fingernails into his soft flesh with a vicious intensity. Gray crud builds up behind his nails. His skin burns red. It hurts, but the pain isn't bad. Avery kind of likes it. He wants to stretch it out, drag it on.

His breath starts coming in little panting gasps. He worries for a moment about filling the shower with swamp fluid and fish/frog eggs, but what comes out from inside him now is the ordinary stuff. White. Pretty as it swirls down the drain with the scales and the slightly bloodied water.

Finally, by the end of his shower, Avery is both clean and rash-free. He wraps a towel around his waist and wishes he could do something about his webbed hands. His feet, he'll cover in shoes and socks, but his hands ... other people will *see* his hands. Avery shudders. They'll see his hands and they'll know him for what he is. Avery's not sure, exactly, *what* he is, but he understands instinctively that he needs to keep it a secret.

It's the wrong season for mittens, and Avery's way too old for mittens anyway. As he pulls on fresh underpants and a T-shirt, he decides to wrap his hands in bandages. He'll pretend he burned them by accident. Avery's clumsy; people will believe that. As a bonus, maybe he can get out of gym.

With his hands bandaged, it's too difficult for Avery to hold an umbrella on his walk to school. To his surprise, he feels fine without it, even though the rain is not light today. The silvery, cold curtain of it is a comfort. It caresses his face. It reminds him of his dream: A person came down from the moon to touch him. To tug at the tides of his untrained body and mold him into something else. He felt like a shifting sea. It was a good feeling.

Avery tries to remember the moon-person's face, but he can't. Water soaks his shirt and jeans and hair. He tips up his chin to catch raindrops on his tongue as he walks along the elevated sidewalk. He thinks about plunging into the deep flooded waterway beside it; he doesn't, but only because that would dissolve his bandages. He shoves his hands into his armpits self-consciously. Gotta protect his secret. Avery has to be mindful, no matter how tempting the call of the depths. He has to be human.

When he reaches the middle school at last, Avery waits a full five minutes before pulling the front door open with the swaddled clubs of his hands and slouching inside. He's late to homeroom, of course, and gets a warning. If it happens again, he'll have detention.

Avery looks over at the back of the classroom where the bad kids and social rejects sit. For the first time, he notices how they're all wearing bandages, heavy and concealing clothes, thick makeup. They're all hiding, like he is. Protecting themselves so they can keep dancing with the moon at night. So no one will find out what's inside them.

There aren't that many, but he's not alone.

IV.

In the flooded world, Rosalie Lacklin is grading papers and pretending she isn't contemplating adultery. She taps her red pen on the top of her desk between marking her seventh grade math students' latest pop quiz. The tapping is in counterpoint to the steady, hollow drum of rain on the roof. Every now and then, Rosalie's eyes dart to the glowing rectangle of her phone, set face-up at the very edge of the desk, then dart away. No. Look out the window instead.

Water traces patterns on the windowpane, but the rain isn't so heavy that Rosalie can't see through. There are the hazy shadows of the houses across the road, as wavering as if they were already underwater. The untrained garden of one abandoned house is a shaggy, monstrous bulk extruding strange filaments of darkness. Rosalie has passed it before, walking; those plants aren't any plants she knows. They're new species for the flooded world, things that thrive with an overabundance of water. Some are almost animal-like, spongy and seeming to breathe.

The full moon is a featureless disk of light through the rain. It makes Rosalie's heart ache, as though an old wound there is coming unraveled.

Her phone chimes. She looks at it, but doesn't pick it up. Her tapping on the desk increases its tempo. She looks back out the window.

Think of the children.

Kurtis Jr., technically a man now but still so shy, so sensitive, so unworldly. Does he have any friends? Has he *ever* had friends? He's very smart, Rosalie knows he is, and very kind, never any trouble to his parents at all, but she's wondered if there might be something a little bit wrong with him for years. Maybe he's depressed. Maybe he's autistic. She wonders if she shouldn't have a talk with him one of these days, make sure he's not too lonely.

Nyleen's not lonely, that's for sure. She's always texting friends, talking to them, even bringing them home sometimes. Rosalie is certain she has a boyfriend she thinks her parents don't know about, someone she's been sneaking out at night to see. Well, she's sixteen. Rosalie was sixteen and in love once, too, and just as sure she was fooling her mother. But maybe she should talk to Nyleen about using protection, about making sure her boyfriend doesn't take advantage—Rosalie chews her lower lip. To tell the truth, her daughter intimidates her a little. She's beautiful, which Rosalie has never been, and confident, which Rosalie has been only rarely. She laughs at her mother's earnestness and concern. Rolls her eyes and smirks knowingly when Rosalie tries to give her any advice. Nyleen has a vicious temper, too; sometimes she yells and cries without warning, shrieks in Rosalie's face that she'll never understand anything, never, never.

Nyleen's wrong, Rosalie thinks. She understands her daughter just fine. It's Avery who confounds her. He's as quiet as Kurtis Jr. and as moody as Nyleen. He's always been a middling to poor student, occasionally getting in minor trouble here and there, but he's been acting out more lately. Ruining his bedsheets by dousing them in noxious water—did he go down to the basement rec room and hold them under the stagnant pool that serves as its floor? Avery is in remedial math, so he isn't in Rosalie's class, but she sees him at school. So many of the kids these last couple years are like him, sullen and fishy-smelling and somehow alien. Maybe it's just puberty. It wasn't like this with Nyleen and Kurtis Jr., but every child is unique.

The idea of approaching Avery about his dirty laundry, or about anything else, fills Rosalie with exhaustion. She wouldn't know where to begin.

Her phone chimes again. Moonlight filtered through rainwater glances off its pale face. Rosalie puts her pen down and picks her phone up. She stares at the messages on its screen. Her heart pounds, and she smiles despite herself.

Think of your husband, Rosalie.

The disease is creeping across his spine and his chest, the way water crept across the roads and valleys and low places of the town when the floods began. Doctors shrug their shoulders. They've seen this before, but they still don't know quite what to do about it. Kurtis Sr. snarls in pain, won't let his wife touch him. He no longer works, but he goes out in the evening and Rosalie pretends she doesn't know where.

Rosalie shudders and squares her shoulders. She taps out a response message, sends it off along the invisible web that connects phones to one another. She deserves this slim sliver of happiness, doesn't she? Doesn't she? Kurtis Sr. is the one who started this, who made their relationship into the cold, rotten thing it has become.

When Rosalie imagines the future, it's like looking down into a fathomless well. It's like staring into the mouth of a deep cave. Kurtis Sr. is dying with their marriage. The world is drowning as his flesh bubbles with corruption. And what if it continues forever this way? Always drowning, always dying. Never ended, never gone. Rosalie doesn't think she could endure that. It's the only thing that might be worse than the loss she knows is coming.

The phone sings out. A time, a day, a question. An image of a heart, throbbing red and pink.

Rosalie stares out the window, as if begging permission from the watery moon.

V.

In the flooded world, Kurtis Lacklin Sr. has a vicious erection. That's the only word for it, *vicious*. It hurts him to get hard lately, but that doesn't stop him. It hurts, but it reminds him that he's still alive, still a man.

His penis burns and stings so much he imagines the skin splitting, the tip leaking blood. He imagines his dick bursting from his fly, tearing through zipper teeth, burgeoning right up to the glass behind which the mermaids do their underwater dances. Right up to Selwyn Kimball.

Selwyn goes by Selena here at the club, but Kurtis Sr. knew who she was from the moment he saw her floating in the tank, and he's never called her anything but Selwyn in his mind. She's so much prettier when she's not pretending to be a boy, though Kurtis Sr. has to admit he likes her more with those testosterone-induced androgynous proportions, with breasts reduced to a pectoral whisper through surgery. Not that he's a fag or anything. Kurtis Sr. likes women, and however much she might try to deny it, Selwyn is all woman. He just isn't a breast man. He prefers them skinny or athletic, with strong jaws and noses.

Selwyn is captivating in her fake fish tail, with her untrained, girlish dance moves. Kurtis Sr. aches more with each undulation of her muscular abdomen, dappled in light filtering through the blue pool water from the top of the tank. Her black hair spirals weightlessly around her face. She teases that she's about to take her top off, and it's exciting even though there's practically nothing there to see, even though Kurtis Sr. is not a breast man.

He leans forward and puts his hand against the glass. Selwyn swims up and meets it with her own palm. They are so close to touching. Selwyn's smile is a knife to wound his heart. Kurtis Sr. isn't a fool—he knows she's smiling because of the generous tips he leaves in the fishbowl with her name on it, and because of the money he pays her for what they do after the show. But he can't help but hope—can't help but *believe*—that she really feels something for him, too. Even if it's only compassion for a dying man who was nice to her a decade ago, when she was thirteen.

The song ends in a crunching flurry of techno-beats. Selwyn blows Kurtis Sr. a kiss and swims for the top of the tank to catch a breath of air. Kurtis Sr. tries hard not to cum in his pants or make a sound of ecstasy and pain. He imagines that there is no cave between Selwyn's legs, no tiny worm, that her bottom half is truly one sleek, scale-dappled green-and-gold tail. That such creatures as mermaids can exist, that they will inherit the earth after the water has conquered it forever, has swallowed up the last boats and bridges. He imagines until he almost believes it.

One more song, one more dance. Then he'll be with her. Then she'll touch him with her small cool hands, tender even through latex gloves. She'll turn his pain into something else. She'll make him feel that he can transform, that he can live in the tidal swells of a drowned planet.

VI.

In the flooded world, Selwyn Kimball is giving a sad, sick middle-aged man a handjob. Selwyn doesn't refer to the man by name in his mind; "Kurtis", to Selwyn, is only ever the man's eldest son, a kind and overly serious child turned quiet, nervous, and alarmingly handsome young adult.

The sick man's naked torso, down to the place where his pubic hair begins, is covered in pustules and veiny reddish-black streaks that remind Selwyn alternately of lichen and of wounds. Selwyn is not disgusted by this, although it makes him pity the man and fear contagion. He thinks his latex gloves, and staunch refusal to do anything with his mouth, will be enough, but a nagging, quiet voice at the back of his brain reminds him he can't be sure. He doesn't know exactly what disease the sick man has. The sick man himself doesn't seem to know.

Selwyn channels his pity into the movement of his hand on the sick man's cock, tries to make it seem passionate and sensitive. The sick man likes to think that Selwyn is attracted to him, that they have a special bond, perhaps that Selwyn would be here in the private backstage room with him even if Selwyn did not need to earn a living. The sick man also prefers that Selwyn not speak, which is fine, and that Selwyn keep his shimmering fish tail on, which is fine except it makes it hard to get from the tank to the private room quickly. The sick man, like most of the club's clientele, either thinks Selwyn is a girl or wants to pretend that he is one. This is not so fine, but Selwyn's learned to tolerate it; this job wouldn't work for Selwyn as a boy. There's no market for that kind of thing in this conservative little town. Selwyn bites his lower lip viciously when the sick man calls Selwyn a lovely little lady, when he compliments the soft and "unmistakable" femininity of Selwyn's hands.

The sick man finishes, weak and watery, with a little gasp. Selwyn's mermaid tail is splattered; that's no big deal, it wipes clean easy. Now that he's done, the sick man has only a sad smile and a wad of cash for Selwyn before he leaves the private room and vanishes into the liquor-scented, moonlit night. If he sees Selwyn somewhere else during the day, behind the cash register at the 7-11 or paddling his little tin canoe through the sunken district, his face will curdle with disgust and shame, and he will act like he doesn't know Selwyn, has never known Selwyn. His wife will look at Selwyn as though Selwyn is a fat leech stuck to her skin, sucking busily away.

Later, nursing a cigarette in the parking lot and looking up at the moon and stars through a haze of barely-there drizzle, Selwyn will feel preposterously sad about this. The sadness will linger, bone-ache, heart-damp, no matter how sternly he tells himself it's stupid. He doesn't like the sick man. He doesn't respect the sick man. Why should it matter if the sick man is embarrassed about paying Selwyn to jerk him off? What would Selwyn even *do* if the sick man acknowledged him in public?

Selwyn will sigh. He'll savor the warmth of the lit cigarette in the cave of his cupped hands. Watch as it burns itself down to a pillar of ash. This is what he enjoys more than smoking, really.

Two women, fellow mermaids, will stumble out the back door of the club in their street clothes. They'll have just gotten off work, too. Selwyn will recognize the tall one with green hair as Anemone. The short one with big tits and hips is called Madison, he thinks; she's new. These aren't their real names, of course, but they're the names Selwyn knows. Anemone and Madison will have their arms around each other, both laughing with their heads tipped back like they're howling at the moon. They'll stop in the middle of the parking lot and share a long, deep kiss.

Maybe that's why Selwyn is sad. Maybe he's feeling the lack of real love in his life. He has no use for real love, he'll tell himself, but the sadness will remain. The desire to have someone to share such giddy, half-drunk feeling with in a wet nighttime parking lot. Someone he'd want to take back to his apartment. Someone young and beautiful, nowhere close to death.

Anemone will see Selwyn and wave at him. "Hi, Sel!"

He'll nod at her and put his cigarette in his mouth, although it will have almost burned away.

Anemone and Madison will continue towards an unknown destination, their shoes splashing and clicking across the asphalt. Selwyn will imagine that someone, somewhere is thinking of him, that the moon from which he took his mermaid name is looking down on him with compassion. But the moon is a great blind eye, rolling relentlessly through the dark, trained on nothing at all.

December Story

The Snow Queen

In the evening when I open my mailbox there is a letter from K. It's hard to tell whether he's in the hospital or not. He must've started the letter there; he talks about nurses, no privacy in the shower, bad food on plastic trays. But the address on the outside of the envelope is written in pen, not crayon. Maybe he's out now. For how long, who knows. K didn't write any dates in his letter or use the word "today." He says he's getting worse and his lips are covered with blisters. He says he's getting better and he was able to walk in the sun; he drank a cold beer under a striped awning.

I haven't seen K in three years. Every time I think he must be out of my life forever, one of these letters comes and I have to remember I miss him. I hate him a little for always peeling back the scab on my heart. He's the one who decided to end things between us; he has no right.

I put the letter down. I open a window even though it's freezing. The air hits my face like the palm of a dead man's hand. Snow swirls around in trains of glitter like tiny stars. K's beer means nothing about when the letter was written; he likes cold drinks in the cold. I wonder if he's out there, walking through the winter with nowhere to go. I imagine him with fingertips dyed blue, in an ice palace beneath the solid surface of the lake.

Before we got together, he used to get tipsy at parties and crawl into my lap. "Let me steal some of that body heat, Gene. You run warm." He hadn't started T yet, so his cheek was very smooth against mine, as well as cool and dry. He felt like a soft-skinned mannequin, not real but not unpleasant. And I let him lean against me until he began to feel human. I didn't realize what he was doing at the time. That he had an ulterior motive, I mean. He made fun of me later for being so oblivious.

I close the window when the air starts to hurt my lungs. If K's outside tonight, he's going to suffer. He might not make it until dawn. I don't want to think about that.

A braver, better man than I am might put on his boots and go out searching. Maybe these letters are a test of my devotion. Maybe K really wants to be found and brought home again. But I don't like the cold, and I'm not very brave. And I remember how K would get when he was upset. It was like his voice was a needle made of ice. He said everything he knew would hurt me most in calm, detached tones. And later he would apologize, but his tone was still calm, detached. There's always been something wrong with him, and love can't fix it. My love can't, anyway.

Gene, the sky is the color of ashes and your eyes. Gene, do you remember the time you showed me the rose gardens?

He never says "I miss you," but it isn't hard to read between the lines.

I think about throwing his letter on the fire, but I won't do that, either. I walk barefoot on the carpet to the bookshelf. I carefully fold K's letter back into its envelope, and I put the envelope in an old cigar box with all the others. I try to ignore the return address in the top left-hand corner.

I sit down at the kitchen table to work on my latest jigsaw puzzle. This one is all different shades of blue. The image is supposed to be two children riding a reindeer, but I can't see it yet. It's just edges. Celestial blankness, corpse fingers, frozen lake. I search a long time for the final piece that will finish the border and close it off, but nothing ever quite fits. None of the shapes fall into place.

A Letter From the Ice Palace

Dear Gene,

I have this dream I'm in a nightmarish mental asylum, like from Bedlam days. I'm naked, and it's so dark I can't even find the ground. There are other people there, but they're all kind of off in their own little mental states. I listen to them breathe but they don't say anything. And I hear heavy footsteps all around us. Something big is coming our way.

I have this other dream, or maybe it's waking life. I'm in a hospital with bright lights and oatmeal-colored walls. I have to ask a nurse to come with me if I wanna shower or take a shit. My lips are chapped and blistered, and the doctors say I'm getting worse. Their drugs say I'm through with pain, but the doctors look at me, and they listen to me, and they look at my mouth, and they shake their heads. I've forgotten what it's like to wear real shoes and pants. Time falls through my fingers like water, and I don't know how long I've been here. Sometimes there's a needle in my arm, and a tube. Unreality flows into me from the tube, branches through my veins and takes me into the dark dream. I'm waiting for the big thing to come and scoop me up in one huge hand and carry me off into the void.

More prosaically, the food here fucking sucks. Not that I eat it half the time, anyway.

Time. It runs away with me caught between its teeth. I guess I haven't written you for a while. I guess maybe you're wondering where I've been. Well, me too.

I'm not sorry I walked out on you. Otherwise, you'd have to deal with me now. Me and my fucked-up mouth. I don't know if I loved you, exactly, but you sure don't deserve that.

I don't know why I'm writing. You never replied to my last letter. You never reply to any of my letters. Maybe it's just for me. It's good, sometimes, to try and get my thoughts in order. It's good to remember I still can.

<hr />

I went under and drowned in the hours. They took the needle out of me and it hasn't come back yet. My lips look normal. And the doctors say I'm better. The drugs say I'm through with sickness, through with want. I sat outside in ordinary clothes beneath a striped awning and drank a cold beer. It was allowed. I let the carbonated chill sparkle on my tongue like snowflakes. The sky was sunny. Then it was gray, the color of ashes and your eyes. I only remember your eyes and your dick and the warmth of your hands. When I look at you in my mind, your face is scribbled out. Except for your stare. When I said terrible things to you. When I left.

A nurse gave me a Rubik's cube to work on. It was all made of ice, no colors I could align, but I had to try and solve it anyway. The edges of the puzzle stuck to my fingers.

Gene, do you remember the time you showed me the rose gardens? I wasn't interested in the flowers, but in the insects crawling through their thickets of thorns. I wish I could've believed in beauty, like you. Instead I wanted to see the truth of the world. I wanted to penetrate the fucking marrow, find out what was underneath all the cruft. I found rot, and then water, and then I fell through the looking glass. It shattered. Pierced my eye and my heart, Gene. That's why I'm stuck in this stupid hospital.

I dreamed a girl came to my window. At first I thought she was another patient; she was so skinny and so tangle-haired. Then I noticed she was wearing lace-up leather boots to her knees underneath a slip dress and an old fur coat. Then I remembered where I was. She sat on the windowsill, half-in and half-out, swinging her legs like she didn't care she might fall.

"Your boyfriend's not gonna come find you, you know," she said.

"I know. He's not my boyfriend anymore, anyway."

"Sometimes the way these stories shake out, the person left behind goes looking. Not him, though. I'm glad. You don't deserve it."

"I know." I squinted, trying to see her face. But it was all in shadow, except for her teeth. "Who the fuck are you, anyway?"

"I'm your worst nightmare, baby." She swung herself all the way into the room and started coming towards me. Her footsteps were big and heavy. I was paralyzed in bed. "I'm exactly what you deserve."

The girl's teeth tore into me. I kissed her the way I used to kiss you, but better.

I was naked in the snow. It shone with blue moonlight all around me. The field was silent. I was alone.

When I woke up, I went to the bathroom mirror to see if my face had changed. My eyes were wide open, staring like you used to stare. I could see no beauty. The rest of me was just an empty shell, an empty house, waiting for something to happen.

Yours sincerely,

K

An Unsent Letter

Dear K,

You don't sound well. I mean, you sound more unwell than usual. Do you want me to come out there and find you? I've been thinking all day today. I think I should find you. I think you need to be found. I feel scared and stupid, planning to show up on my crazy ex-boyfriend's doorstep and—what? But I love you, K. I love you still. Or I'm haunted by you, at least.

Your last letter had a return address I didn't recognize. I finally looked it up online. Do you have your own place again? Are you living with someone? Why didn't you mention him, or her?

You said you were waiting for something to happen. You were sleepwalking, having night terrors. It sounded like the same night terror, actually, from that first time you let me stay over at your place—well, I guess it was the only time you let me stay over at your place. You didn't remember anything in the morning, so I've been carrying it alone.

When I asked why we had to sleep separately, you laughed and said you were a nightmare to share a bed with and you were doing me a favor. You offered to take the couch, but I insisted, even though my feet dangled off the end and the middle sagged so my back sank into it like synthetic plaid quicksand. I thought you'd counter-insist when you saw me that way, force me out of those swampy cushions and march me to your bedroom and make me lie down between your crisp sheets. A considerate person would have. Instead, you laughed again.

"If I were Procrustes, you'd be cut off at the ankles," you said. You turned out the light and left.

Sometime in the early hours, the door to your apartment creaked open. I woke up right away. I'm a light sleeper to begin with, and it was impossible to get comfortable on that couch. There you were, wearing your long wool coat even though it was too early in the year for it. Your feet were bare. I assumed you were awake and heading out on some secret business. I followed you as quietly as I could. I was worried. I was curious. I was a little mad, maybe.

We traveled down the middle of a road without cars or other pedestrians. Moonlight flashed white on your heels. The hem of the coat slapped the backs of your knees. The first few fallen leaves skittered across old asphalt. Eventually, you left the road, crossed the sidewalk, and crawled under a derelict chain-link fence. On the other side of the fence there was nothing but a small, narrow vacant lot thick with vines and garbage.

As I struggled to climb the fence, being too big to crawl beneath it, you tipped your head back and screamed at the sky. It sounded like a rabbit caught in the mouth of a wolf, or a trap. You screamed and screamed, not seeming to breathe, standing rigid and still. It was like you were just an object for the scream to pass through, a flesh radio.

I vaulted over the fence in a panic. It cut my hands, and I scraped my knees when I fell heavily to the ground, but I didn't care. I ran to you, grabbed you up in my arms, turned you around. You were still screaming. I saw that you were naked underneath the coat. I saw that your eyes were closed. I'd never seen anyone sleepwalk before; I hadn't really been aware it was something that could happen in real life. Your eyeballs were flickering rapidly under the thin pale lids, making their icy lattice of tiny blue veins jump and twitch. Your mouth was a wet black pit of sound. The only other noises were the breeze and the last of the summer cicadas. I was sure someone would come out and see you, see us. Someone would call the police.

I didn't know what to do. I grabbed your shoulders and shook you, hissed at you to wake up. A drooling string of blood crept from the corner of your mouth. My heart jumped as I thought of internal bleeding, but then I saw how your lips were chapped; the skin had split around their edges. You opened your eyes and they looked bloody, too, filled with red strings. I almost thought something had gotten inside them, some irritant. But the screaming stopped, and your body drooped between my hands.

It seems incredible to me that a person could be in that state and just forget about it the following day. How many times has this happened to you, K? Do you know? How often do you remember?

I suppose this means I might have had similar terrors before and never realized. But I always wake up where I fell asleep, and nobody who's lived with me has ever said anything. Then again, I never said anything about it to you. Until now.

"Gene?" you muttered. "Where am I? What happened? Was I fucking sleepwalking again?" I'm paraphrasing, of course, but I remember the "fucking." I said you had been, and I told you I was going to take you home. I asked if you thought you could go under the fence again, or if you wanted me to try and boost you over it.

"I'll go under," you said, yawning. Your bare chest heaved so I could count your ribs. "But where's that girl? Did you see her? Who was she?"

"What girl? You were alone the whole time, K."

"No," you said. "There was a girl. She threw a rock at my window. She was wearing tall boots and a fur coat. I think she had too many teeth. She wanted me to come with her."

That part isn't paraphrased. I remember it exactly. It freaked me out.

"You were dreaming," I said. "Forget about it."

We struggled back across the fence. We returned to your apartment, my arm around your waist, your head on my shoulder.

After that, I never tried to sleep in the same bed as you. But when we lived together I'd often lie awake, staring at the night-gray popcorn ceiling of my little room, listening for you. I wanted to be there to bring you home if you ever wandered out again. I wanted to save you from the girl with too many teeth, or whatever made you scream.

You only walked in your sleep once in those years that I know of, and that was just to the refrigerator. I found you standing in front of it with the freezer door wide open, blasting arctic air into your placid, dreaming face. You didn't wake up when I led you to your futon.

I'm sorry.

I should have reached out much sooner. You hurt my feelings, and I was a coward. I didn't understand how much you needed me. I didn't want to let myself understand. I'm still upset with you, but I'm going to make sure you're safe.

The Devil's Looking Glass

He's on the doorstep in those stupid red boots of his, the ones that make him look like a six-foot-two kindergartener. I love them and I hate them. Their toes are crusted with crisp snow, and he stomps it off in the space where a welcome mat is supposed to go. I've never had anyone I wanted to welcome, so I left it a square of concrete that's a slightly different gray than the concrete around it. I can smell that concrete from all the way up here, and the snow, and the boot leather, and Gene's sweat under his scarf and hat and puffy coat. My mouth starts dripping. He's a marshmallow man. My spit burns holes in the ice, freezes translucent at the end of the branch I'm perched on.

Gene knocks on the door. He doesn't know the house is empty yet. He presses the doorbell, which never worked in the time I lived there and doesn't work now. He waits a moment, shivering, then knocks again. Again, again, again.

"K?" he calls in little clouds of warm breath. "K, are you in there? I got your letter. I've gotten all your letters."

Within the house, nothing but tomb-silence. I put sheets over all the mirrors I didn't break. When my face finally changed, I didn't want to look anymore. I saw beneath the skin, finally, in waking life. I saw that a building is just another kind of cell. I solved the puzzle, and I won't go back.

I didn't think Gene was the going-back type, either. The girl with the fur coat and the sharp teeth was right about a lot of things, but she wasn't right about that. He took me by surprise. It's lucky I was hanging around near the place I used to live, a ghost outside a body. Even wild animals can become attached to their cages, enough that they have a hard time leaving when freed. I returned to the hospital four times in three years.

I kept some pieces of the mirror I shattered, the first one that showed me my new face. (I looked like, and unlike, the girl with sharp teeth. I looked frozen, blue. I looked like I was past living anywhere.) That's lucky, too. I'm holding one of them now, a thin, shining knife with strips of old shirt wrapped around one end for a handle. Blood always slides right off it. When I use it to look at Gene's reflection, I see him eyeless, shivering, his hair starting to thin on top. I see his blood under the skin, rushing out of his heart to warm his long nose and elegant cheeks. I see his teeth blunt and square behind his lips. I see how it's no different to feed a tangle of roses, a knot of worms, a man's mouth. Everything beautiful comes out of something disgusting; every disgusting thing is potentially beautiful; nothing, ever, is painless or safe. I hope Gene understands that someday, that he can come to it from the opposite side I did. He needs to let the horror in.

Maybe I can help him understand. Maybe I can finally show him what I feel, plain and direct, instead of speaking or writing it in words that only reach him as bitter slights.

He's done waiting at the door now. He's walking around back, looking for a way in. The trees are bare at this time of year, and I'm not so very high. If he just turned his head towards the sky, he'd see me.

I grip the slice of mirror and point its tip at him.

"Hello, Gene," I say. "I missed you." My voice sounds flat and scratchy, hardly a voice at all. It could be the wind in the oaks and birches. But he startles, he breathes in sharply.

"K! Is that you?"

I don't know, Gene. Is it still me? How long since it's really been me?

He looks up.

Gorgonland

"The air smells different in Puglia," Caroline told him before they left. "It isn't like the air anywhere else. There's an herbal quality to it."

That is certainly true—it has a salty, crisp, chlorophyll-tinged scent. Dominic isn't sure what makes the air smell that way, or if its smell is as unique as Caroline claimed, but it doesn't at all resemble the way the air smells in London. Or in New York. Or in the other places he's visited during his twenty-six years on Earth so far. Not that he's visited so many places. Caroline—wealthy, British, widowed, twice his age—wants to change that.

When he first got together with Caroline, during the brief time she lived in Manhattan, several of Dominic's friends assumed it was a sugar mommy relationship, at least in all but name. "I'd play straight for that kind of money, too," Alan said. "There's no shame in it."

To which Dominic reminded his friend that he was bisexual, and insisted—truthfully, he believed—that his attraction to Caroline was entirely sincere, and had nothing to do with the fortune her husband had left her. Alan, like all of Dominic's friends, remained skeptical until he actually met Caroline.

Although she looks younger than fifty, she doesn't really look *young*. That hardly matters; she's beautiful. She was a model in her twenties, and it's still obvious in her tall, thin body, her graceful but rigid bearing, her finely chiseled face. Her hair, once dark blonde, has frosted over with silver in an extremely flattering way. She has lines on her forehead, which she covers with a fringe, and more lines around her mouth and eyes; these are so delicate that they're almost invisible unless you're standing very close to her, or she becomes upset. Caroline rarely allows herself to become upset.

Her eyes are enormous, their color hovering between green and blue. Not unlike the Ionian Sea, Dominic told her, when she showed it to him. The comparison earned him a kiss on the mouth. Above them, palm trees reached for heaven. Seagulls soared. They stood on a walkway of marble, lined by flowers Dominic couldn't name. That was in Taranto.

A worm of nebulous dissatisfaction was gnawing its way through Dominic even then; he ignored it. Continues to ignore it. He's an extremely lucky man. He has nothing to complain about whatsoever.

But now, in Lecce, on the iron-banistered balcony of their palatial rented flat, the worm's activity has become more urgent. Dominic feels restless, frustrated for reasons he can't pin down. Anxious, almost. As absurd and melodramatic as it sounds, he has a sense of impending doom.

Maybe it's the architecture. All the buildings in Lecce are made out of beige limestone, so it looks as if the entire city was carved in its entirety from a single rock, crafted in one piece. On top of that, a lot of the historic cathedrals and such are covered in baroque flourishes: acorns and flowers, leaves and garlands, saints and angels and long-dead important men, all lovingly chiseled out of the same local limestone, all the same color. Dominic doesn't know much about art, or history, but he doesn't think he cares for the style. It feels oppressive.

Earlier today, down a narrow side street, he saw a dog lying beside the entrance of a building. The dog had very pale eyes, almost yellow. The dog's fur was a dusty, warm color—the same color as the doorway. Dominic was sure it was a stone dog until it moved. It startled him.

Caroline's arms twine around his waist. Caroline's lips brush the back of his neck. "What are you thinking?"

He can't tell her. She doesn't really want to know.

"The stone here is beautiful. I'm impressed with all the carvings on the churches, how they haven't worn down that much."

"Lecce stone is very soft when it's first removed from the earth; that's why they were able to make such detailed, smooth carvings. But it hardens with time, as it's exposed to the air, and that means it doesn't deteriorate as quickly as other soft stones."

"Oh. That's interesting." Her hands are sliding underneath the waistband of his joggers.

Out in the city, fairy lights and throngs of people. Up in the sky, star-pricked darkness. The hardening air and its herbal scent.

Caroline's dry laugh. "It isn't that interesting."

They don't speak more until morning.

———

Dominic dreams of Medusa. She's not a green sexy lady with boa constrictor dreadlocks. She's the old, old Medusa, the one he saw painted on ancient pottery in a museum in Taranto. (Puglia was full of Greek colonies before the Romans had their day, said the English language tourist brochure.) Medusa has a beard made of writhing, skinny black snakes to match the mane of snakes on her head. She has tusks and a snout like a boar. Her eyes are huge, crazed, full of fire.

Medusa stalks the empty beige streets of Lecce. Dominic and Caroline are hiding from her. Or rather, Dominic is hiding. Caroline doesn't seem to notice that anything's wrong. She keeps stopping to consider a rose garden, a fluted column, a necklace of opals and coral in a shop window.

Medusa's shadow falls over the jewelry store and the stores beyond it. Medusa stands at least thirty feet tall. Dominic knows exactly what she looks like. He knows he cannot look directly at her. His heart rate leaps.

"Caroline, please, come on. We have to go. She'll catch us."

"I find the choice of materials gauche, but I must admit the craftsmanship is spectacular. What do you think? Shall I try it on?"

"Caroline, she's almost here." He pulls her arm. He wants to run.

"Dominic, please. Stop being such a child."

"Can't you see her shadow? Can't you hear her footsteps?" The hot, meaty stink of the shadow's breath fills his nostrils.

"Of course I can. But really, you must learn to live with these things."

"We have to get away!" He really is like a child. Hot flush of shame as he realizes he's close to crying.

Medusa doesn't talk. She doesn't growl, or roar, or anything. Apart from her footfalls, she's as silent as a fossil. Only her shadow, her smell, her movement shaking the ground.

Caroline looks at Dominic with sea-colored eyes. Such calm waters. But he can't tell what's beneath them. "My dear, what makes you think one can *get away*?"

The shadow deepens. Dominic stares at Caroline.

Caroline turns her eyes upward.

—◇—

In the morning, Dominic does his workout routine on the stone floor of their rented living room, 16th-century stone ceiling arching above him like he's in a tiny cathedral all his own. He does sit-ups, push-ups, squats, hand weight exercises. Normally he'd listen to music, maybe a podcast, but right now all he wants is the harsh rasp of his own breath. He is a scrap of flesh inside a stone egg. He's a soft thing in a shell. There's something clean and austere about it. His sweat, his breath, the stone, the silence.

He feels better, he thinks.

There's a strange dust piled in the corners of the room, spread in dunes and drifts beneath the windows. A yellowish dust. Sour moonrock. Dominic thinks the flat ought to be cleaner, given the amount of money Caroline's paying. But when she comes in to eat her breakfast and he points out the dust, she just laughs at him.

"It's natural," she says. "It's from the stone. It sheds in summer."

"Like an animal," says Dominic, disconcerted, and Caroline laughs at him again, so he doesn't say anything else. It's not mean-spirited laughter, or at least Dominic is almost sure it's not; she doesn't mean to make him feel stupid. Maybe she doesn't even think that he's stupid.

"Thank you for bringing me here," says Dominic. "I'm learning a lot."

"Every young person deserves to see the world," says Caroline. "Roger took me around the world when I was young." Roger, her dead husband. He was in his fifties when Caroline was nineteen, an inexperienced model fresh out of a council flat. Caroline doesn't talk about Roger much, or about her past; Dominic wishes she would. Maybe then he'd feel more like they're equals.

"It would be a shame if you rotted away in Brooklyn your whole life," says Caroline, and she squeezes his ass as he passes her on his way to the kitchen. "The world deserves to see your beauty, too."

Dominic knows that Caroline wouldn't be interested in him if he was much older, if his body wasn't tall and slim and toned, if his face wasn't chiseled and symmetrical. He tries not to resent that; after all, the same is true of every male partner he's ever had. After all, the same was doubtless true of Caroline's partners, when she was young and poor. It was doubtless true of Roger.

Maybe someday, Dominic thinks as he prepares himself a smoothie, he will be a middle-aged man with a lot of money. Maybe Caroline will be dead, or otherwise out of the picture. Maybe he'll meet a handsome twink, or a beautiful girl, decades younger than he is. He'll buy that youth and beauty with luxury. With favors. He'll try to mold him, or mold her, in his own image. Isn't that the way these things always go?

The smoothie is almost the color of the Ionian sea—the shallow parts, where it's a lot more green than blue. It's almost too pretty to drink.

"Dominic?" calls Caroline from the other room. "Darling? Will you join me for breakfast?"

Of course he will. He loves her. It's ridiculous to feel upset. He's on the most glamorous vacation of his entire life with a wealthy, gorgeous, sophisticated woman who dotes on him. Who spares no expense. He'd be insane to feel dissatisfied, to get an itch for leaving.

"One second!" Dominic gulps the smoothie. It tastes like kale and Puglian air. The dust lies on the kitchen windowsill. It makes him think, for some reason, of yellowed teeth. Teeth ground into powder.

———◇———

At the table, Caroline keeps fidgeting with the rings on her left hand. She keeps clutching and unclutching the handle of her mug, fluttering her long fingers. It's uncharacteristic of her, so Dominic asks if something's wrong.

"It's nothing. My hand's a bit stiff, that's all." She smiles at him. "You'll understand when you're as old as I am."

There's a small pile of yellowish dust between the salt shaker and the pepper mill. Dominic looks up at the ceiling, trying to catch sight of a slow downward trickle. Nothing. The dust might as well have spontaneously generated itself on the table. After breakfast, he sweeps it into his palm and dumps it in the trash.

———◇———

Another cathedral: Dominic startles at the dog standing, alert, head cocked, by the massive arched door. It's the same dog from the other day, he's sure of it. Pale-furred, pale-eyed, the color of Lecce stone. Only when he gets slightly closer, he sees he was mistaken. This dog *is* stone. Carved at the base of a twisting tree full of fruit. On the other side of the door stands a stone angel, sword in hand.

Caroline leads him inside. The cathedral has a crypt they're going to see. Dominic thinks he knows what a crypt looks like. He's picturing stone shelves lined with skulls, long white leg bones organized in rows, wall-mounted torches and more carved archways.

Instead, the crypt is more like a cave beneath the cathedral with a mouldering pile of brown bones dumped in the middle of it, like a pile of shit from some gigantic animal. There are metal barriers and velvet ropes to keep visitors from touching the pile. A skull sits toppled on the ground near Dominic and Caroline, almost touching the metal grate. Dominic looks inside the empty sockets of its teeth.

"I wonder who that used to be," Dominic says. "Like, probably some monk, I guess. Right?"

"It doesn't matter who any of them were," says Caroline. She sounds distracted, remote.

Dominic doesn't speak to her again until they leave the cathedral, and he turns to see Medusa blazing out above a side entrance, her gargoyle face carved from beige stone. Just like the Medusa on the vase in Taranto.

"That seems like a strange thing to put on a Christian building," says Dominic, pointing.

"Why's that?"

"Medusa's not exactly in the Bible, is she?"

Caroline laughs. "I suppose not. Well, those ancient motifs stayed popular for a long time around here. I think she's supposed to ward off evil spirits. Something like that."

Dominic shudders. "She's warding *me* off."

Caroline rolls her eyes lightly. She takes his hand. "Come on, then. Let's go home for a siesta."

They don't sleep in the hot afternoon. Instead they fuck, Caroline on top, lights out, sharp spears of golden sunshine shooting through the blinds and landing across their bodies. Dominic holds her hips, looks up at her silver-blonde hair shaking over her shoulders.

He thinks how beautiful she is, and then he thinks of other people, and then he stops thinking of other people and thinks of nothing at all. His orgasm is just a little blank space before fatigue washes over him. And the spears of sun.

He looks up at the vaulted ceiling. The bedroom has all these carvings that Dominic thinks look like butt plugs; Caroline says they're supposed to be rosebuds. Usually more of a Sicilian motif, she says. They represent potential, she says. New growth. Youth. But they're carved from old, old stone, and they will never bloom.

When Dominic and Caroline return to the front room, the living room, there's yellowish dust piled high on the table. Covering the top like mounded sand. Falling over the sides with a soft, dreadful sound.

There's been no apparent damage to the walls or ceiling; it's unclear where all this dust could have come from.

Caroline's mouth is a narrow line. Dominic's is an O.

"This is bad," he stammers, after several long moments. "I knew I was getting creepy vibes from this place. I don't think it's safe here."

"Don't be absurd. It's just a pile of dust. It can't harm you."

"It's unnatural. We should go." Unreasoning panic. Dominic knows he's being a child. Why does he feel such dread? It's not the relationship. It can't be the relationship. But maybe there's something wrong—very wrong—with this rental flat.

"The owners really should have warned us how *much* dust would come off the stones in summer. This is rather grotesque." Caroline turns to Dominic. She sees something in his face. The dread, he assumes.

"Oh, darling." She strokes his cheek with a cool fingertip. "Don't overreact. I'll clean it up so it can't bother you. Then I'll make a phone call. I'm paying to stay here. This won't do."

The dust falls over the sides of the table, sand in an hourglass. Dominic turns away. Best and easiest to let Caroline take care of everything. How lucky he is to have a partner who can take care of everything.

But maybe, if he plays his cards right, he can convince her to stay somewhere else.

There are a few buildings in Lecce not carved from the beige limestone. New buildings, modern, in different parts of the city. They're not as atmospheric as this one, not as rich with history, but they're nice, some of them. Classy. Expensive-looking. Caroline sorts of places.

———✦———

This evening, though, Dominic can't press matters. The dust incident has put Caroline in a bad mood. She cleaned it up, and she made her phone call, but the owners' response to her complaints was unsatisfying in some way—she won't go into detail for Dominic. "I don't want to think about it any more. It's not for you to worry about, either. Let's go shopping, and then to dinner. Seafood tonight, I think. Unless you'd care to try *pezzetti di cavallo*."

"Sure," says Dominic. His Italian is virtually nonexistent, but he recognizes the name of the dish—it's horse meat. He doesn't think Caroline knows he knows. Sometimes she likes to feed him exotic, mysterious meals and only afterwards reveal that he's been chewing balls, or blubber, or brains, or bear. As though she thinks he's squeamish about what he puts in his mouth. He always puts on a show of scandalized astonishment, because it so clearly pleases her. Tonight, he wants to please her.

Between shopping and dinner, a homeless man jumps into the road in front of them. He has a sleeping puppy, still at the age where it looks more like a fuzzy overgrown potato than a dog, tucked under his left arm. He gesticulates with his right arm while saying something in Italian. He's younger than Dominic, and he would be handsome if he had a shower, a haircut, and some new clothes.

Caroline makes her face blank and hard. She looks through the homeless man and pushes right past him. Almost knocks him down, and his puppy, too.

He says more in Italian. He makes a hand gesture Dominic definitely recognizes. His breath smells like hot, sour fruit. He looks a little bit like Dominic, actually, like they could be related. They're the same size, with the same wavy black hair and prominent Adam's apples. The puppy is still asleep.

"I'm sorry," says Dominic. "I'm American. I don't speak Italian. Uh, *mi dispiace*."

The man grimaces and shakes his head. He says something else in Italian, but his anger seems to have dissipated.

"Okay," says Dominic, nodding and shrugging like an idiot. "Okay. Sorry. Okay. Everything's cool now?"

The man nods and shrugs back. Melts into the shadows of a nearby alleyway. Puppy safe in the crook of his elbow.

——◦——

At the four-star restaurant, horseflesh and tomato sauce sliding down his throat, Dominic wonders why the homeless man wanted their attention. He wonders whether Caroline understood what he was saying. She claims to "barely" speak Italian, but to Dominic it seems like she knows the language rather well. She has little chats with their waiters when they go out, asks questions about the food.

He can't quite bring himself to ask her about it. Across from him, she swallows her own horseflesh. Delicately swabs up sauce with a slice of thick bread. She still seems annoyed. Her blue-green eyes are almost yellow in the dim, flickering light of the chained-up lamp swinging above their table. The furrow between her eyebrows casts a harsh shadow. Maybe the homeless man said something to offend her? Something misogynistic, or just mean? Maybe the homeless man said something about Dominic?

He thinks about hardening with age. He wonders whether, after fifty years exposed to the open air, after thirty years living with wealth, Caroline has simply reached a point where she can't feel sorry for anyone who causes her inconvenience. For anyone who's beneath her station, and not useful. Even if that person has a really cute puppy.

Maybe that's what will happen to Dominic one day. He searches himself. Is he all right with that? Can he just let it happen? Does he have a choice? Would he be strong enough to go back to eking out a living in Brooklyn? Would he be stupid and sentimental enough?

"You're not drinking the wine, darling," says Caroline. "I'm sorry; do you not care for it? I know you've said reds sometimes give you headaches. This is excellent, though, I promise you."

"No. Sorry. It's really good wine; I'm just off in my head a little." Dominic takes a long sip from his glass. It *is* really good wine.

"I got it especially for you." Caroline turns the bottle around on the table so he can see its label. Beneath the name of the vineyard, an ink drawing of Medusa, the old Medusa, bearded and tusked and goggle-eyed. Blazing out at them like a wrathful angel.

———————

When they return to the flat, Caroline is rather drunk. Dominic should be too, since he ended up drinking more than she did, but he feels remarkably clear-headed. He perceives everything in sharp detail, but there's a slightly abstracted remove to these observations, as though they're all happening in a movie he's watching instead of in real life.

He turns on the lights, and the living room is filled with yellowish dust. It's all across the floor, the table, the TV, the trendy low-slung chairs in front of the TV. It's a carpet, a blanket. An even, quarter-inch-thick coating.

Dominic feels like he might throw up.

Caroline doesn't seem to notice anything's different. She slips off her satin pumps and lets them rest in the small pale drifts of stone dust. She leaves bare footprints across the lunar floor. "I need to sleep." Yawning. Light tread up the short, less dusty stone stairs.

Dominic can't think of anything to do but follow.

Maybe in the morning, when Caroline sees all this new dust, it will bolster his request to change flats. She'll agree that they should leave. It won't be any trouble.

———————

In his dream, they haven't returned to the flat yet. They're still walking the nighttime streets. The stone walls garlanded with fairy lights, the palm trees looming, the city like a dollhouse miniature, a different breed entirely from megalopolises like London and New York. The crowds on the stone, on the marble, on the brick paths all speak a language Dominic doesn't understand. He only understands their cigarette smoke, their laughter. Caroline droops against him, slight but warm and solid.

They enter an alleyway, black and redolent of rotting fish. Flashing eyes of a half-dozen cats. Wrong turn.

When Dominic backs them out, hurriedly, the crowds of people have vanished. The fairylight-twinkling streets are silent. Except for the thunder of footsteps: a massive body approaching. Much closer than Dominic would have thought possible. How did he miss those footsteps before? That huge silhouette, darker than the sky behind it? His heart jumps.

He tugs Caroline's arm. "It's her again. We have to go. Come on." Fear clutching his throat like a bony hand. It's a wonder he's able to speak at all, and he's proud of how cool the words come out. Manly, firm.

But Caroline slips her arm from his grasp and steps away.

She looks into his eyes. She's actually a bit taller than him in her heels, so she looks down at him. Her eyes are like the sea in the dark. Indigo ripples with shining peaks. Caroline isn't drunk at all. Why did Dominic think she was drunk a moment ago?

"Wouldn't it be terrible if I died and left you back where I found you?" she says, with a faint smile. "Or, what if I died and left you all my money? Would that be worse?"

"Caroline, please—"

The footsteps shake them both. Dominic stumbles. There's movement in the air above them. He thinks he can smell Medusa's breath.

"What if I turned to stone, Dominic, my darling? What if I lived for another fifty years? What's the outcome you fear most?"

"Stay with me!"

Her face is suddenly grave. "No." A light rustle of her stiff, cool fingers through his hair. "Now run away if you want to live."

Dominic knows he should be brave. He should be unselfish. He should be loyal. He should save her, or at least stay with her. But Dominic wants to live, and he's already running as quickly and quietly as he can back down the alley that smells like rotting fish. There's a wall low enough to vault over at the far end. There are shadowy palm trees beyond it, and a few faint stars.

Behind him, neither Medusa nor Caroline makes any sound.

———◇———

He wakes up sweating. Panting. Clutching at the soft, thin white bedsheets. Stone dust trickles across the rumpled fabric like a system of tributaries. It's still the middle of the night.

"Caroline," says Dominic. " Caroline? I had a really weird nightmare."

He knows she'll be annoyed he's woken her for this, but right now, he needs comfort. That sense of dread has returned, and it feels absolutely bottomless. "You were in it."

He puts his hand on her slim, bare shoulder. It's shockingly cold and smooth. Hard and lifeless as a piece of carved stone.

The Mood After All

Neely Parker was the first person I ever kissed, but she'd been dead for nearly ten years when I finally brought her home with me.

To be clear, Neely was still alive when we kissed. We were both fifteen, taking the same remedial Spanish class the summer before tenth grade. She had short hair bleached the color of a highlighter, and she was the only girl in our high school who didn't shave her legs or armpits, at least as far as I knew. She liked to flaunt the dark down with sleeveless dresses that reminded me of my mom's porcelain doll collection. I had a crush on her the moment she first asked me if I had a light, which I didn't, and then invited me to smoke with her under the bleachers anyway.

I don't think she ever had a crush on me back, not really. We were friends that summer, and she could see the little cartoon hearts in my eyes whenever she turned my way. Maybe she felt bad for me. Maybe she was just curious what would happen. But one day, as she was smoking a joint under the bleachers and I was pretending to smoke it but not actually inhaling, she turned to me and asked if I wanted to make out with her a little.

I was stunned into silence for a second. Then I managed to squeak, "Sure".

Neely tasted like weed and the inside of a mouth. Her tongue ran across my teeth and she bit my lower lip. I touched her breasts over her checkered, lace-fronted dress. They were very small, and she wasn't wearing any bra. I felt like I was inside and outside myself at the same time, and I wanted nothing more than to keep going and going until we both tumbled into something I could not imagine, but could feel gathering in my lower belly like a mass of lightning-studded clouds.

We didn't. After maybe five or ten minutes, Neely pushed herself off me and smoothed her ratty lace. There was dirt crushed into her bare knees.

"Sorry, Scout," she said. "Guess I'm not in the mood after all."

I flinched a little, surprised; I'd only started being called Scout a couple weeks before. When someone used the new name, it always felt a little like there might be a secret third person in the room, a real Scout I'd never met. Almost everyone still called me A_____ until I reminded them not to.

"It's okay," I assured her. "I'm not really in the mood, either." I was lying, of course. But I think she believed it.

We never fooled around that way again. Neely never brought it up, and, because I was scared of ruining our friendship or seeming uncool to her, neither did I.

After that summer, we were never in the same classes. We saw each other in the halls at school, but we drifted apart. Neely moved out West for a while after graduation, and I went to State. We didn't stay in touch. I didn't even think about Neely much until five years later, when she died.

I was home with a BA in English, living with my mom and working at a 7-11, struggling to write a novel and trying to feel that my life was still on course, that it was all going somewhere.

I'd broken up with my college girlfriend the previous winter, and although it was late summer now, although I'd initiated the breakup, I was still in mourning. I thought of her constantly. I'd think of her until I couldn't take it for another second and my mind flung itself past her into older memories, other lost loves: the girl to whom I'd lost my virginity, the boy I'd had a brief fling with before Shana and I got really serious. Bruce Springsteen, circa the cover of *Darkness on the Edge of Town*, who I'd had a secret crush on—and secretly wanted to be—all through elementary school. And Neely Parker.

I read the obituaries in the local paper every morning, a morbid ritual I've kept to since my parents still lived together and my dad would recite them out loud to me in silly voices. The day Neely's name appeared on the obituary page, it felt like I'd summoned it. My guts lurched.

When you're in your early twenties and you've led a sheltered life, it doesn't occur to you that people your own age can die. Not people you *know*, anyway. You're aware, intellectually, that it's possible, but only in the way you're aware that the sun will eventually become a red giant, or that your body sheds tens of thousands of skin cells every year.

My hands shook on the newsprint. The tiny Neely-face printed next to the obituary still looked more or less like it had at age fifteen. Her cheekbones were sharper. She had a few more piercings. Her hair was a slightly different style, but it was still fried neon blonde. I realized I had no idea how old the photo was. It could've been taken a couple months ago or a couple years ago. Maybe she had changed more by the time she died.

The obituary was short. Neely'd moved back in with her dad after a year out West. She'd had a lot of "struggles." Reading around the euphemisms, I gathered that she'd been having problems with drugs and/or drinking. Mental health issues, maybe depression or bipolar disorder. The obituary didn't say how Neely had died; between that and the list of "in lieu of flowers" organizations to which it was suggested mourners donate money, I was pretty sure she'd either OD'd or committed suicide.

I felt an enormous heaviness. The backs of my eyes ached. I would have given anything for Neely to have a second chance at life in that moment. I would have opened my own veins to bring her silver-studded, smirking, smoke-scented face up out of the grave.

Then the moment passed, and I closed the newspaper, and I ate my eggs, and I went to work.

I assumed, of course, that I'd never see Neely Parker in the flesh again.

A little over a month ago, this assumption proved wrong.

I am now the assistant manager of the 7-11. I'm still struggling to finish my first novel. I have my own apartment, which I shared with a partner until the forced 24/7 togetherness of the 2020 pandemic quarantine trashed our relationship. They fled as soon as they could, and they took the cat with them to Buffalo. Which was fair enough. He was their cat to begin with. At any rate, when the dead started coming back, I was lonely.

You remember, of course. This spring, along with the rising crocuses and daffodils, dead people started turning up on their loved ones' doorsteps. At least in certain parts of the United States, my own included.

The dead people don't seem to be dead anymore. Even those who died years ago aren't rotting. They breathe. They have pulses. They look healthy and whole. They don't sleep, and they don't need any food, but besides that, they're physically alive.

After all the strangeness and turmoil of the past few years, it wasn't in the news for as long as I'm sure it would've been in, say, 2010. Once we'd established that the returned weren't flesh-ripping zombies, and that most dead people in most places were still staying dead, the articles and news bulletins and opinion pieces slowed to a trickle. Twitter's trending topics moved on to other things: some new celebrity outed as a rapist, a political scandal, the schadenfreude *du jour*.

But the resurrected remained. Most of them are people who died young, or at least young-ish. All of them are people who still have living loved ones: parents, spouses, siblings, children, ex-partners, best friends. These are the ones they appear to, turning up in their yards or kitchens or bedrooms looking just as they did before the hit and run in 1975, or the AIDS in 1989, or the overdose in 2003, the drowning in 2014, the bullet in the chest six months ago. Whatever it was. They come to people who never emotionally recovered from their deaths and to people who put them to rest in their hearts long ago.

The resurrected never explain where they've been or why they're here, at least not as far as I know. I've heard that many of them seem almost normal at first, that they retain their personalities and respond to most stimuli. They seem a little sleepy, that's all, maybe a little drugged or hungover. Tired, listless, confused. So I'm told. They might linger in that state for hours, days, weeks, just going through the motions of their old lives. Trying to reintegrate themselves into families that look at them in moist-eyed disbelief or in wary, quiet horror. Skimming books, watching TV, phone-scrolling through social media, doing crafts, exercising. Preparing meals they don't eat. Lying awake in their old beds or on guest room futons all night. Maybe fucking.

Eventually, whatever the case, they all slow down. They talk less and less. Unless prompted, they move less and less. Occasionally you see them walking around like open-eyed somnambulists, a truly living person leading them gently by the arm through a parking lot or a lawn's long grass. After a while, they don't move or speak at all, no matter what anyone does to encourage them. They stand or sit frozen, blinking, breathing, unresponsive. Living statues. Living corpses.

That's the state Neely was in when I ran into her dad at the dump. He had brought her there intending to leave her. He was carrying her awkwardly, like she was a department store mannequin. He was crying. He looked so old that I wouldn't have recognized him without Neely in his arms, her bleached hair swaying over a placid, perforated face the color of milk.

"Mr. Parker?" I said. I was getting rid of some mildewy sofa cushions.

He blinked and squinted at me behind his smudgy glasses.

"It's me, Scout," I prompted. "I was ... I was friends with Neely in high school. I came over to your house once. You let me have a donut."

"Oh." His already wrinkled forehead furrowed more. "Scout, yes. Of course." I couldn't tell if he actually remembered me or not.

"So," I said, staring pointedly at Neely's frozen form, "what brings you here, Mr. Parker?"

"Listen," he growled through gritted teeth. Sweat beaded his balding scalp. It was a sunny day. Light bounced off Neely's facial piercings and spangled the trash-strewn dirt. "You have no right to judge me for this. You have no idea what it's like to ..."

"I'm not interested in judging anybody," I interrupted. My voice came out sounding calmer than I felt. My heart pounded. I saw Neely's half-lidded green eyes blink slowly, once. Her dark lashes scraped the deep shadows beneath them. A fly buzzed around her lips, which were just barely parted, exposing her large front teeth. One of those teeth was chipped at the bottom, which it hadn't been when I'd known her. Still, she looked so young. She *was* so young, I supposed. Twenty-three.

I'll be thirty-three in October.

"I'd like to make you an offer," I said to Neely's father.

I would have given him money, but Mr. Parker let me take her for free. It felt wrong, he said, to sell his only child, even if she was long dead, even if she was a soulless shell of the person he'd lost. I wondered why a man who'd been perfectly willing to leave her to stand forever or slowly rot a second time among the trash heaps of the county dump was suddenly demonstrating scruples, but of course I said nothing.

With effort, I got Neely's body to bend into a sitting position. She was rigid, but she wasn't unyielding. Her flesh felt soft and warm. I buckled her into the passenger side seat of my car, and I drove her home. To my home. Our home, now.

I know what you might be thinking, but it wasn't a creepy sex thing. That didn't cross my mind—okay, maybe for an odd moment or two here and there, but the thought never stuck. It would have been rape, and arguably necrophilia. Besides that, it would've been profoundly unsatisfying: like screwing a co-matose woman, or a RealDoll. Sure, some folks out there are into that stuff. I'm not. I like my partners alive, moving, and enthusiastic.

Like I said before, I was lonely. Like I said before, I felt sorry for her. All the emotions I felt the day I read her obituary came back in a rush when I saw her father dragging her through the dump.

Neely Parker was beautiful, and wild, and funny, and an excellent kisser. She deserved more than the dreariness of an American public school education followed by drug addiction and despair. She deserved a longer life. If she'd had the chance, I doubt she would have wound up managing a 7-11 in our shitty hometown.

When I got back to my apartment, I moved Neely to an armchair in the living room that the cat had liked to curl up on. I tried to get her into a position I thought would be comfortable. If I ignored her open eyes and her strange rigidity, I could easily pretend she was just asleep. Her breath smelled stale but sweet.

I took a step back to examine her in a more leisurely manner. Neely was wearing cheap, ripped black leggings and an oversized T-shirt that read DIRTY DICK'S HOUSE OF CRABS. Her clunky boots were patterned with small purple flowers. One boot had pink ribbon laces, the other black leather. That detail seemed the most like the Neely I'd known. Her skin was blemishless. No track marks, if there'd ever been any. No slashes on her wrists, if there'd ever been those.

"Well," I said to Neely, "I'm going to make myself a sandwich. Settle in. Let me know if you want anything."

She didn't. Of course.

The next day I went to Thrift Town and bought Neely a bouquet of new-old dresses, the kind she wore all the time when we were fifteen. Dressing her up was actually much easier than moving her to the car and then the armchair had been. Maybe whatever unknowable awareness remained in Neely's resurrected husk was softening her limbs, making them easier to manipulate. Maybe she was thawing under my care. Maybe she remembered, too, and wanted this.

Or maybe I was just getting better at knowing how and where to push and pull.

When I was finished, she wore a sleeveless dress made of some silk-like material, with a short, full skirt and a zipper up the back. It had a diaphanous ruffle around the neckline. It was a cool green that matched her eyes and complimented the brown of the armchair. Her old clothes went in the garbage, except for the boots, which went next to my shoes on the mat inside the front door. Her bare feet were narrow, blue-veined ivory carvings.

I brushed her hair out of her face and sat her with her hands in her lap. The effect pleased me. She looked so alive. Her eyes seemed brighter. I could have sworn I saw the corner of her mouth twitch.

It felt so nice to have another person with me, waiting patiently for me when I got home from work, breathing softly in the dark as I fell asleep (I moved Neely to a smaller wooden chair in my bedroom at night). I changed her clothes. I even did her makeup the way I remembered it—thick wing-tipped eyeliner and shiny lip gloss. I watched YouTube tutorials until I was sure I could get the eyeliner right. I talked to her.

Sometimes I thought she moved when I wasn't looking. It was never enough that I could be sure, but it often seemed that her hands or feet had shifted slightly. Some days her face looked very sad to me, and others pensive, and others mischievous, and others simply blank—although I couldn't have pointed to any particular thing that had changed about the set of her features. Sometimes I thought I heard rustling, a silky skirt sliding over itself, when my back was turned.

I didn't admit it to myself, not then, but deep down I grew increasingly certain that Neely was slowly coming out of her stupor, that one day she would wake up and become herself again.

Sitting cross-legged on the floor in front of her armchair, I told her everything I remembered about her. I asked her what had happened to her, how she'd died. I waited as long as I thought it might take her to answer the question, and I nodded gravely like I was listening to speech instead of the low whirr of a window-mounted air conditioning unit.

At first I didn't tell anybody at the 7-11 about Neely. Then, after a couple weeks, when Clark asked if I was seeing anyone, like dating, you know, in a romantic type way, I said maybe I was.

He asked who.

I told him he didn't need to know.

But I didn't take it back.

I did my work. I ignored other people to the extent I could get away with it. I drove back to my place and got stuck in traffic on the way. I ate a microwave spaghetti dinner sitting across from Neely, thinking about that day we kissed, that day she called me Scout when the name still felt like something brave. I hadn't done anything brave since high school, apart from bringing Neely home.

She seemed to look right at me with a steady gaze. There were no incipient worry wrinkles on her forehead. I'd gotten kinda fat over the years; she was, if anything, thinner. But not by much. I wondered if the bleach would ever grow out of her hair, if I'd ever have to re-do it.

I felt a warm flush spread from somewhere deep in my stomach out through my entire body. Just as if I really were in love with Neely, as if she were really my new girlfriend, as if I were happy with a secret.

The dark was thick and soft as fur. Little granules of color swarmed in front of my eyes as I tried to make out what was happening in my room, why I'd woken up.

"Scout," said a woman's voice. It might have been Neely's voice. I realized in that moment that I couldn't quite remember what she'd sounded like. "Be still."

I felt a small, splayed hand pressing down on my chest. I couldn't move. I couldn't even blink. I could barely breathe.

My eyes adjusted to the darkness a little and I saw Neely crouched on top of me, her face in shadow. Her hair and her dress almost glowed. Her hand on my chest was like anyone's hand, warm and trembling. She tilted her head and shifted her shoulders, and now I knew beyond a doubt that she was looking at me. Really looking at me. I felt the mattress sagging beneath us. I heard her breath.

I wanted to ask her how she'd come back. I wanted to ask her what it was like being dead. I wanted to ask her whether she knew why she'd been resurrected. I wanted to ask why she'd drawn into the shell of herself, refused the life she'd been given. I wanted to ask if she was going to leave me now.

My mouth was as paralyzed as the rest of me, but Neely seemed to hear the questions anyway. She leaned down until her face was right up against mine. I could smell her breath, sweet and dirty and tinged with smoke.

"You want there to be reasons," she said. "There aren't, or if there are, I don't know of any. Death is a hole you fall down and keep falling down forever. Death is when everything stays the same for you all the time. You don't move forward anymore. Only farther down the hole." Both her hands stroked my chest now. My naked skin shuddered into goosebumps.

"You can't help me, Scout. You don't even know who I am."

I wanted to protest that I knew her a little. That I'd thought about her a lot. That I'd love the chance to get to know her better. To have gotten to know her better.

"Oh, Scout," she whispered. "You dumbfuck." Then she kissed me. Her mouth was dry. She didn't taste the way her breath smelled. She tasted like nothing at all. Still, my body responded as much as it could. If I'd been able to move, I would have pressed myself into her, twined my tongue around hers.

After a few seconds, she broke away and wiped her lips on the back of one hand. "Sorry," she said. "I guess I'm not in the mood after all."

She rose and climbed off of me, off the bed. I still couldn't move. I couldn't even turn my head to see her after she stepped outside my field of vision.

I wanted her to come back. I wanted her to rip me open, to suck blood from my neck, to take my life for her own. Anything. Any form of climax. Anything but dismissal, anything but walking away.

The dark, the little granules of color. The sound of light footsteps moving steadily through the door, down the hall, into the living room.

The click of the lock on the front door. The door opening softly, closing softly behind her.

Nothing.

I still couldn't move.

Sleep.

———

When I woke up the next morning—this morning—I was only half-relieved to see Neely still sitting in the small wooden chair beside my bed, just where I'd left her. It had just been a dream, a hypnagogic hallucination—I've had those off and on since I was a kid. Sleep paralysis, you know. It always feels very real while it's happening.

Neely was still with me, but that meant she hadn't spoken to me after all, hadn't revealed herself. She remained glassy-eyed, statue-blank, and porcelain-doll pale. In the slanting lines of sun through the blinds, her skin and hair looked white like the wing of a moth. White like a maggot.

I reached out to touch her on the shoulder, and her flesh was very cold.

My stomach lurched. I realized I couldn't hear her breathing at all. She wasn't breathing. When I pressed my fingers to her wrist, my ear to her chest, I found no heartbeat.

I couldn't deal with it. I left her in the bedroom. I brushed her hair and did her makeup beforehand, like I always did, though I couldn't bring myself to change her clothes.

When I got home in the evening, she'd already started to stink. Summer around here gets brutal. You know.

That's why I'm here, at the dump in the middle of the night. I didn't know where else to take her. She doesn't have a grave I could put her back in, just a plaque on a wall. Her dad had her cremated the first time around; the obituary said her ashes were scattered out around the lake. And the lake is too far away, too long a drive with someone rotting in the trunk of your car. Or the passenger side seat, because even now, I don't think I could bear to put Neely in the trunk. Also, I read once that throwing human corpses in the lake is really harmful to its delicate freshwater ecosystem, or what's left of its delicate freshwater ecosystem after a century of pollution.

If this place was good enough by Mr. Parker's estimation, I guess it's good enough by mine, at least now that she's truly, finally dead again. It wasn't that difficult to sneak in after hours. Maybe I'll get caught on a camera or something. I don't really care if I get caught; everybody in town knows about the resurrected dead. You catch glimpses of them the way you used to catch glimpses of deer in the early morning. People might think I'm a ghoul, but they won't think I'm a murderer. I've done nothing wrong.

She's getting puffy already, and her skin's started to go mottled. Kinda veiny. Flies all around her head like a crawling black halo. It's not Neely anymore. It's not anybody. As far as I know she's the first resurrected person to die again, but I guess someone had to be.

I wish it had been different. I wish I had a better story to tell you.

All I know is that her future and mine are both garbage. Look at the news: the fires and storms, the plague, the fascist armies, the guns and the poverty and the no-good-jobs-anywhere, enough crap to leave the walking dead an uninteresting footnote. I have as good a life as I'm ever going to have; it's nothing like I dreamed it would be when I was young, and it gets smaller every day. Maybe Neely had the better idea, getting out early. Maybe that was the best she could do. Or maybe she came back because it wasn't, and it was up to us, up to me and her dad and the whole world to help her live again. And we failed her. Or it just wasn't possible, not anymore, not now.

Maybe it's my fault. Maybe if I'd understood her enough, she would've shaken off her death and shared my dreary life at the end of the world with me. She couldn't save me and I couldn't save her. But maybe, if I'd gotten it right, we could have rotted together.

Or maybe everything Neely told me in the dream was true. Maybe there's no reason for any of it. Things come and go, they happen and they fall away, and it's all sound and fury, signifying nothing. We just have to deal with it as best we can, caring for our memories, going to work, burying and re-burying the dead until they stay in the ground and our own hearts finally stop.

Lupus in Fabula

It's the smell that wakes me up: iron, wet earth, fur. Not raw, twisting bodies. Not smoke and hot fat. My eyes open. I'm lying on my back. I hear breathing beside my ear. I turn over to see a wolf looking at me with bright yellow eyes, panting as it lies beside my head on a bed of leaves and pine needles. Its black lips are pulled back in a kind of smile, teeth bared. It's not growling or snarling, just staring at me. It looks more like an animal than a person now, but it still has those yellow eyes, like headlights caught in the dark night sky; they're glowing starkly and they're so very sharp; they're cutting into my brain.

I feel trapped under this wolf's gaze. I can't move. My heart pounds even harder than before—it seems to be shaking the ground beneath us both—and then everything gets very slow and sticky but super-clear. It's hard to be surprised when the wolf rises and, gently, starts to bite my clothes off. Cotton and cheap windbreaker fabric tear and I watch my summerdark skin with its blackheads and cellulite emerging from their woven ruin, a neglected and pitiful landscape. The wolf's nose leaves a cold, moist trail between my ribs. I wait for its mouth to bite down.

———◦———

I shouldn't have gone out tonight. Everyone knows not to go out tonight. You're supposed to stay inside your house once it's dark and not even think of the woods. The beach. The moon. No matter what scents and sounds filter through your walls and windows, you don't go outside. You don't even step out on your porch for a smoke. You make yourself a cup of tea and you watch something anodyne on TV. You put in earplugs and go to bed early, and you make a point of not remembering your dreams.

I'm not a child, or some thrill-seeking teenager. I'm not a fool. I don't have a death wish. But something seized me, and I knew I could not rest until I found out what happened on the beach each year. Now I know. I'm falling out of my own head, out of my cowardly body, into a gray pit, and I still can't bring myself to regret the knowledge.

———◦———

We run: my sibling & I down the sand for sheer joy, splashing in nightfoam, singing to the big moon. Sibling's eyes gold fire. The smell of ashes swirling over our shoulders.

———◦———

Time breaks like a wave or a smashed glass. This story is happening all at once, all within each moment of itself. There is no order of events where I'm going, in the shape my wolf will lick out of me.

———◇———

When its tongue starts tugging the pink tissue of my inner mouth, I gag. My teeth grow, and they itch. I worry the roots will be exposed. For a few years, I had recurring dreams that my gums peeled away from each of my teeth until they dropped into my bathroom sink like ripe, tiny fruit. Those dreams made me unsettled. No one I spoke to about the dreams could tell me what they really meant.

My girlfriend at the time said the dreams were probably about feeling I had no control over my life, but that wasn't true. I was already planning to cut her loose.

I haven't been touched this way since the aftermath of our last argument. I haven't had parts of someone else's body inside mine. I haven't been inside anyone but myself. Now, with the lather of saliva spread over my naked chest like ointment, I can get outside my head. I can see through wolf eyes. I can see this scene playing out from above, like I'm floating near the ceiling of the cave.

———◇———

It isn't hard to find the secret ceremony. I haven't had to be clever, or sneaky, or even all that careful. It's on one of the beaches, the one that's a little dark sand valley surrounded by humble hills instead of high cliffs. Super convenient; it means I just have to keep low to the ground on top of my chosen hill, and I'm invisible. It's night, of course. The sea whooshes and the cicadas whir, and I'm not really that far from the action.

There are about twenty of them, I think, gathered around a big pyramidal driftwood bonfire. Different shapes and sizes. Different skin colors. All adults. All naked, or almost naked, although some of their bodies confuse me. Slowly, I realize each person is wearing a cloak made from the skin of a single animal.

I stare and stare, looking for a distinctive tattoo or a familiar pattern of moles, but I can't recognize anyone from town. I've lived here since I was thirteen, so I know pretty much everybody. Still, I can't say for sure any of them aren't my friends or neighbors or co-workers, either.

The cloaks are made of all different hairy mammals, not just the deer that live around here. Wild beasts, no dogs or horses. Mostly carnivores. But there's an anteater, its huge claws wrapped around the waist of an androgynous figure, its boneless, narrow head dripping between the person's small nipples. Its fanlike tail sways from their hip, brushes the sand like a broom. There's an ape—an orangutan, I think. There is one deer, antlers spreading like bleached branches. The man beneath the antlers is arm in arm with someone wearing the pelt of a gray wolf.

Their skins have ragged, still-wet edges. I can smell them from up here. I don't doubt for a moment that they're the real thing.

Their skins under their skins glisten with milky drops of sweat, or maybe some kind of ointment.

In the shadows farther from the fire, a hulking, shaggy shape pounds its hands on a large, simple drum. A woman with the sleek, babyish face of a seal or sea lion pulled over her human eyes and nose blows into a woodwind instrument that looks carved from bone. The sound is reeds and tumbling stones, whistling wind and thunder, the sea and some lonely bird.

In this town we have a saying: "The wolf in the story comes when he's called." Same idea as speaking of the devil, but I've never heard our version anywhere else. I was admonished with fables about wolves a lot when I was younger and nosy, gossipy. I outgrew the gossip, but not, I suppose, the nosiness. My nostrils are always twitching at spoor in the air.

Underpaw, soft granules of earthstuff. The hunt in my nose I run to catch warm grasseater the game we dance we chase—my howl & the howl of my sibling a holy braid of sound. Leap through a tangle of moonsoaked smell brambles clutching fur claws splash and we chase chase chase. Foaming the prey's mouth. Smile and circle. A high, thready bleat.

———◇———

The moon watches with a ruined stone face from the mouth of
the cave, and I think I'll be stuck here forever, entwined with
a wolf, not quite one thing and not quite another. We are in
the center of a story. I have always been circling this moment. I
have always felt this way, joints pulled out of their sockets, back
arched high in pain and ecstasy. Snout gone sharp and crowded
and long.

———◇———

Tear the body, belly, fat muscle organ meat slipping down
my throat, wet bursting salt and iron in the mouth, swallow,
gulp, play. Throw into the air; catch between teeth. Shake
hard, growl. Intestines spilling on the soft ground smelling
good—shitsmell bloodsmell sweetsmell. Roll around in it all.
Prey smiling beneath fanged off hair skin flesh, new face moon-
white, licked clean.

———◇———

Slick stalactites drip and glimmer with dim moonlight on the
high dark ceiling of the cave. I can't see them well, but I know
they're there: dozens of swords hanging above me as my body
quakes. But the wolf doesn't bite, doesn't rip me open, doesn't
eat me. Instead, it starts licking my belly. Not the way a dog

licks, to show submission, but with slow, deliberate purpose. Its tongue is long and smooth, and it makes me itch. My skin feels like it's crawling with insects or bubbling with hives. I'm hot and goosebumped. I'm inside and outside my body as the wolf draws its tongue across my navel and darts between my thighs. It lathes me and molds me. My flesh shifts like a viscous liquid beneath it. Ripples and recedes and remakes me through wolf spit and sweat.

———

Mom said it was a local myth. She told me people tied any gruesome or mysterious or disruptive thing that happened at the right time of year back to an imaginary cult ritual. My manager once described it as "a bunch of delinquent kids setting off fireworks and mutilating small animals." My best friend in ninth grade said it was a select few matriarchs and patriarchs of old backwoods families in the area, handing down a tradition from time immemorial, hexing newcomers and interlopers and anybody they just don't like.

———

After the dreams of my teeth falling out, after I broke up with my last girlfriend, I started to have dreams of dancing. I danced on the beach as the tide came in, and I danced through mud in the woods. I danced on a long board studded with needles and pins until my feet looked like strawberries, and I loved it.

In the morning, my wolf helps me tear off my new pelt. It hurts, though I'm able to do the last part with my own teeth, tasting my own blood and raw red flesh. Underneath my skin I'm human again, with the same body I had yesterday. I look like I've been baptized in a slaughterhouse. I look newly born.

I roll up my skin and look around. I know I'll need it next year. Probably the safest thing is to take it home with me. I've lived alone since Mom died last autumn. I see I'm in a strand of oaks that's a little way inland, but not more than a mile from my house. I recognize it from hiking, from playing truant in these woods when I was in high school.

My wolf regards me with that yellow stare. Its bushy tail wags slowly, and its tongue lolls. Then it turns and sprints off through the trees.

"Wait!" I call, but I don't follow it. I don't move. The air is pleasantly warm and salty on my naked skin. The early light and leaf shadows turn the world a mellow, calming greenish gold.

My wolf darts between trees until I can't see it anymore, even though I feel like I should still be able to. It's lost somewhere between the oaks, the low dark bushes, the tumbled piles of gray rock.

The people in skin cloaks are dancing in a wobbly, seething circle. The erratic firelight makes a confusion of all their limbs, all their faces, all the empty, hollow faces of the skins. I feel like they're all looking straight at me, even though I can't see any of their eyes. The men and the women and the strange ones in between. The leopard and the wolf and the bear. The others. I can feel them gazing at me from their frolic down in the sandy valley, beside the soft black sea, sight cutting through the darkness and spotlighting my small body in the tall grass, behind the crooked tree. My legs are dead, numb, asleep from all the not-moving I've been doing. For how long now? I don't dare stir.

At first, when the dancers start changing, I think it's just the firelight. Dirty brightness and unstable shadows can turn an overbite into a long snout, can turn a man's freely swinging member into a barbed club or give a woman a hairy devil's tail. Then I hear the crunch of bone reshaping itself, the screams, the groaning and crying. They overwhelm the drums and that terrible high flute or recorder.

I see flashes of exposed living meat in the glow of those unsteady flames. I see and smell flashes of dripping fat and spilled bowels and veins braiding themselves wildly through the air, oily-wet tendrils, steaming and smoking. The veins dive back under the beast-skins, which flow over each dancer like something more than clothes. Like empty but living creatures swallowing their innards back up. Taking their revenge on humanity. You wore us; now we'll devour you.

Teeth shine white and wet as pearls. Red, yellow, silver, gold. The screams are dying down, crushed into an array of grunts and growls and snarls by new throat shapes. I see yellow eyes, fire-eyes, looking right at me with dilated pupils. Not down in the valley, but near, more than halfway up the hill. I smell salt and blood. I smell urine as it rivers through my jeans, into the sandy dirt beneath my numb legs. My heart races ahead of my ribcage, ahead of my frozen muscles.

———

Next year, next year. I have to pick the lock of my own back door. I lost the keys with my clothes. Next year, I'll find out who all the rest really are. I'll get to the bonfire early.

I wash both my skins off in the shower and blood goes down the gurgling drain like chocolate syrup in an old black and white horror movie. Next year I'll dance, and maybe none of it will hurt so much.

I throw up in the shower, and there are chunks of raw meat in the vomit, there are small or shattered bones, there's some kind of animal eyeball with a sideways ungulate pupil. My throat burns, the way it burned the first time I tried smoking. I wipe my mouth, thinking of how nothing ever ends, thinking of things I can get used to. Next year, I'll ask my wolf some questions. I'll get the anteater's phone number.

When I'm dry, I put the meat chunks and the eyeball down the garbage disposal one by one. I bury the bones in the garden, under my mother's long-neglected roses.

My sweat glands are vanishing. Coarse hair is erupting from tender places on my palms. We move together in the close, salted dark of a full moon midsummer night.

Content Warnings

Biological Reality: gender dysphoria, traumatic pregnancy

Appetites: animal harm and death (rodents, cats, dogs)

Swallow Me (W)hole: suicidal ideation, self-harm

Therianthrope: rape, intimate partner violence

Leavings: N/A

The Witch's Wife: death of a spouse, self-harm

Close Encounter: N/A

The Holy Incubus of West Virginia: N/A

Desire in the Flooded World: sexual relationship between adult and minor, misgendering

December Story: institutionalization

Gorgonland: N/A

The Mood After All: mention of overdose and suicide, death of a child

Lupus in Fabula: reference to animal mutilation

Acknowledgments

I write a lot about dysfunctional families and very lonely people, but I'm extremely grateful for the support of my own family and the close relationship I've been able to have with my immediate family plus many members of my extended family. I would not be a writer without the encouragement, help, and influence of my grandparents, my aunts and uncles, my cousins, my parents, my brother, and my sister.

I'd like to thank Clarissa Pattern for some insightful feedback on "Gorgonland," and John Thompson for instrumental suggestions on "December Story." Major thanks to Sadia Bies for the amazing cover art.

As always, thanks to my partner Flann.

Publication History

"Biological Reality" was originally published in Warning Lines magazine.

"Appetites" was originally published in Tower magazine.

"Therianthrope" was originally published in *The Book of Queer Saints*.

"Leavings" was originally published in Ligeia magazine.

"Close Encounter" was originally published in beestung magazine.

"The Holy Incubus of West Virginia" was originally published in *Bonemilk*.

"December Story" was originally published in *Mooncalves*.

"Lupus In Fabula" was originally published in Apparition magazine.

About the Author

Briar Ripley Page writes short stories and novellas, including *Corrupted Vessels* and *The False Sister*. Originally from Appalachia, he now lives in London with his partner, two cats, and other family members. *Lupus in Fabula* will be his first full-length collection.

Other Books from Cursed Morsels Press

The Nightmare Box and Other Stories
by Cynthia Gómez

A young queer man finds love at a magical clothing shop—and the courage to stand up to the homophobic cops. A witch who makes custom nightmares wonders why all her victims are connected to the Black Panthers—and who she's really working for. A soon-to-be father encounters a mysterious hitchhiker who tries pulling him back to the days of his violent past. A brand-new vampire, freshly hired at the blood bank, delights in her heightened sexual desire and superhuman strength.

Cynthia Gómez's debut collection is a magic-soaked love letter to Oakland, brimming with feminist rage. Its twelve stories center ordinary people—Latine, queer, working class-as they wield supernatural powers against oppression, loneliness, and dread.

Why Didn't You Just Leave
edited by Julia Rios and Nadia Bulkin

It's the question asked of any story about a haunting: *why didn't you just leave?* But if accounts of people who have stayed in haunted houses are any indication ... it's never that simple.

In this book, you'll find twenty-two all-new stories about the reasons people *don't* leave scary situations—parents who stay in haunted houses to protect their children, convicts who literally can't leave their prison, retail workers who need a paycheck even if it's from a haunted workplace, trauma survivors suffering from agoraphobia, and more.

Featuring Shauntae Ball, I.S. Belle, Die Booth, Max Booth III, Christa Carmen, Raquel Castro, Alberto Chimal, Gabe Converse, Lyndsey Croal, Victoria Dalpe, Alexis DuBon, Corey Farrenkopf, Cassandra Khaw, Joe Koch, E.M. Linden, Steve Loiaconi, R. Diego Martinez, J.A.W. McCarthy, Suzan Palumbo, Tonia Ransom, Rhiannon Rasmussen, and Eden Royce. With illustrations by Luke Spooner, Yves Tourigny, and Yornelys Zambrano.

No Trouble at All
edited by Alexis DuBon and Eric Raglin

Politeness is the glue that holds society together. We are all expected to do our part—a pressure ripe with horror. Rotten, even. Whether we adhere to this contract or defy it, there are consequences. These fifteen stories respond to promises made for us, promises of compliance that cost too much to keep.

Featuring Nadia Bulkin, Shenoa Carroll-Bradd, Ariel Marken Jack, Gwendolyn Kiste, Avra Margariti, J.A.W. McCarthy, R.L Meza, Marisca Pichette, J. Rohr, Simone le Roux, Angela Sylvaine, Nadine Aurora Tabing, Sara Tantlinger, D. Matthew Urban, and Gordon B. White.

Bitter Apples
edited by Eric Raglin

Cursed Morsels Press presents tales of teacher horror from Corey Farrenkopf, Emma E. Murray, Cynthia Gómez, Christi Nogle, D. Matthew Urban, Eric Raglin, and Aurelius Raines II. These writers have worked in the profession, and while their stories are fictional, the darkness they explore is all too real.

In *Bitter Apples*, you'll find students' ghosts haunting classrooms, desperate teachers joining cults, zombies plaguing underfunded schools, and more. The institution of education is rotting. How will we survive its horrors?

Shredded: A Sports and Fitness Body Horror Anthology
edited by Eric Raglin

Reader beware! This sports and fitness body horror anthology is dangerous. Side effects include monstrous steroid transformation, concussion-induced madness, possession by jock ghost, death by yoga cult, and more. Read with caution!

Featuring seventeen reps of terror by Nikki R. Leigh, Tim Meyer, Brandon Applegate, Red Lagoe, Caias Ward, RW De-

Faoite, Mae Murray, D. Matthew Urban, Charles Austin Muir, Joe Koch, Michael Tichy, Rien Gray, Robbie Burkhart, Eric Raglin, Matthew Pritt, Madeleine Sardina, Alexis DuBon, and J.A.W. McCarthy.

Antifa Splatterpunk
edited by Eric Raglin

Fascism didn't die in 1945. Its grave was only temporary. Rising again, this undead ideology shambles into the present, gathering power and spreading destruction wherever it goes.

This monster stalks the pages of *Antifa Splatterpunk*, in which sixteen horror writers explore fascism's many terrors: police wielding strange bioweapons against the public, white supremacists annihilating their enemies through dark magic, and TV personalities vilifying all who defy the rising fascist tide.

But these stories are resistance: Nazi-killing demons, Confederate-slaying witches, and everyday people punching fascists in the teeth. Among the gore is a glimmer of hope that one day this monster will return to its grave and never rise again.

Forthcoming Cursed Morsels Releases

Shaky Pictures of Vanished Faces, a horror and Weird fiction collection by D. Matthew Urban. Coming spring 2025.